DEATH COMES QUICK

Longarm shot him before he could get the pocket derringer all the way out.

The man landed spread-eagled on his back a few paces away, staring back up at Longarm with a petulant expression, as if he'd been punished for just trying to have a little fun.

Longarm said, "Yep, I never meant to let you go. But I wouldn't have gunned you if you hadn't made me, just now."

The figure didn't answer. Men seldom did when they'd been shot in the heart . . .

D0790816

— TABOR EVANS —

LONGARM

AND THE ARKANSAS AMBUSH

JOVE BOOKS, NEW YORK

LONGARM AND THE ARKANSAS AMBUSH

A Jove Book / published by arrangement with
the author

PRINTING HISTORY
Jove edition / December 1991

ISBN: 0-515-10733-6

Jove Books are published by The Berkley Publishing Group,
200 Madison Avenue, New York, New York 10016.
The name "JOVE" and the "J" logo
are trademarks belonging to Jove Publications, Inc.

PRINTED IN THE UNITED STATES OF AMERICA

10 9 8 7 6 5 4 3 2 1

LONGARM

AND THE
ARKANSAS AMBUSH

Chapter 1

It seemed a swell time and place for a combined wedding and bank robbery. The time was late greenup. The place was Aurora, Colorado, a short, lathered pony dash to the depths of downtown Denver to the west, and *then* find the money or the good old boys who took it if you're so smart.

The wedding had been planned for some time by Miss Sara Sue Warren and her gun-toting kith and kin, not with a view to aiding and abetting grand larceny but to end the free fornications of Flypaper Fred Quinn off the Rocking Y. They were getting hitched at First Congregational, down to the far end of Aurora's short main street, at high noon the Saturday after payday, if old Flypaper Fred knew what was good for him, the sweet-talking and slow-marrying son of a bitch, after which the best damned shivaree and anvil shoot the tiny town had ever held was planned to send the happy couple off to honeymoon down by Colorado Springs in a real hotel with indoor plumbing and all.

It being a Saturday the bank only had to stay open until the very hour of the wedding. So they'd posted a sign the day before, warning one and all to get in, get it over with, and get on down to the church no later than eleven-thirty, lest they find the bank door shut in their slugabed faces.

U.S. Deputy Marshal Custis Long, better known to friend and foe alike as Longarm, had no business at either First Congregational nor Grangers' Savings and Loan, as far as he knew. He was fixing to mount back up and ride right back to Denver, as annoyed as he ever allowed himself to be with a member of the unfair sex who wasn't actually pointing a gun at him. As she tried to convince him he should stay, the frisky redhead who'd once run the Aurora post office was rubbing the muzzle of a possibly more deadly weapon against the front of his pants, through her lightweight and loose-fitting calico housedress, pleading, "You have to believe me, Custis. You know how many times our post office has been held up, out this way. Have you already forgotten how you saved the U.S. Mail, and me, and all the fun we had, ah, celebrating?"

As they stood just inside the screen door leading out on her back porch Longarm resisted the impulse to thrust back at her with his own hips; it wasn't easy, as he patiently and not unkindly replied, "I remember you quitting as postmistress and getting married shortly thereafter, ma'am. I still rid out this way, the more fool me, when I found your message waiting on me this morning at the Denver Federal Building. I figured a married woman who'd been held up by post office robbers in her misspent youth might have just cause to call the law as you just did. But, as I just now told you, I've called on both your town law and the new postmaster and you ought to be ashamed of your horny little self and cut that out."

She rubbed against him harder, and might have kissed him if she'd been tall enough to get up under his mustache against his will, as she insisted, "I swear I've seen at least two faces off those wanted posters I still see every time I post a letter and sort of jaw about old times at the post office, Custis."

2

He shrugged and replied, "Them woodcuts on reward posters leave a heap to one's imagination, even when the engraver traces a real photograph caresome. We nailed all them post office robbers the last time you got this forward with me, and I sure wish you'd calm down, ma'am. Your town law says he hasn't noticed any sinister strangers of late and since I just returned from yonder post office I can assure you there's nothing in the safe worth all this fuss, this weekend."

She hugged him tighter, buried her red head in the tobacco tweed folds of his ready-made three-piece suit, and skillfully gripped his dawning erection with her love lips through all those layers of wool and calico, as she sobbed, "Oh, Custis, I'm all alone and so afraid."

He couldn't help remembering how much better she could do what she was doing with nothing at all between them. But even if he hadn't been officially on duty until noon there were things a man did and things he just didn't. So he let a hint of steel creep into his tone as he told her, "I know how alone you'll be 'til no sooner than say Wednesday, ma'am. The town law mentioned that business trip your new husband left on. But what are you afraid of? It ain't true that playing with ourselves leads to insanity. If it did we'd have all been locked up in insane asylums by now."

She played with him some more as she protested, "He's not all that new and I was a fool to wed a man so much older than me, given my warm nature and natural needs. What's the matter with *your* natural needs this morning, damn you? I know you want this. I can feel how much you want it and you just said, yourself, we have until at least Wednesday to satisfy these old yearnings, darling!"

He chuckled dryly and replied, "I doubt any man could satisfy you this side of suicide. I told you the last time I was trying that my job made it tough for me to spend much time with any one gal in particular."

She pouted, "You spend more time with a certain widow woman who dwells in a big brownstone by the state capitol

3

than you ever spent with *me,* the way I hear tell."

He sighed and said, "I reckon that's what I get for leaving certain back doors after sunrise but, for the record, the lady of whom we speak so cruel ain't got a husband coming back to her this Wednesday or any other, the poor cuss. So I thank you for the suggestion and with your permission I'll be on my way."

The somewhat younger and smaller but surprisingly strong redhead clung to him like a love-starved limpet as she insisted, "One time! Just lay me across the kitchen table, hoist these skirts, and prong me hot and hasty just for old times' sake! I swear I've had a long tub bath since the last time I did it with anyone else and you know what they say about a slice of mince pie tasting just as good, once the pie plate's been washed nice and clean, no matter who might have et off it last."

Longarm repressed a shudder and removed his pancaked Stetson long enough to bestow a chaste, brotherly kiss on her fevered brow. As he'd hoped she mistook his intent and relaxed her grip on him just long enough for him to disengage and make it out the screen door. Another young housewife was hanging baby diapers in the next yard over. She seemed to find it amusing when the redhead called him all those names from her own back doorstep. Then he was out in the alley and legging it back to the center of town.

In a town the size of Aurora this didn't call for much legging. It was little more than a crossroads settlement, handier to the surrounding cattle spreads and truck farms than the more serious ride into nearby Denver for simple goods and services.

He'd left the livery nag he'd ridden out from Denver with the boys at the volunteer firehouse just this side of the bank. They'd warned him he might find his mount tethered on the north, shady side if they had to go out on a call. With that wedding all set for any minute now, they were short-handed, whether the anvil shooting went right or not. Most of the volunteers would be attending the wedding and shivaree in their good clothes with the avowed intention of disturbing the friends of hell and making the harpers of heaven miss a measure and hang on to the horns of their clouds.

Longarm was just as glad he'd be out of town before they fired the fool anvils. Folk always expected any man sporting a badge to do something when human life and property got damaged, federal or local, and firing anvils tended to get damaging indeed.

Opinion seemed divided as to which old country the tradition had originated in. It was popular as all get-out in the American West. It took advantage of the square mounting hollow in the base of your standard hundred-pound anvil. The blacksmith courting the rep of a good old boy on, say, New Year's Eve, the Glorious Fourth, or a shivaree sunk one anvil into the dirt out front, upside down, and filled that hollow with blasting powder, say a couple of measuring cups' worth, then fused it with another anvil standing atop the loaded one, right side up and poised for flight when the charge between 'em went off with a bang that was considered a fizzle if it didn't rattle windows over the horizon. The sun was almost directly overhead now. Longarm knew he was fixing to hear them fire them anvils no matter how far he'd ridden by noon. He still figured it would hurt his ears less if he was closer to Denver. So, seeing the firehouse doors were still gaping, he commenced to walk faster. That suggestion the redhead had just made about that widow woman on Sherman Avenue had been a good one. He'd be off duty as well as stiff as a poker by the time he made it back to downtown Denver.

He and the firehouse were on opposing sides of the street, since he'd naturally clung to such shade as there might be on his way from the redhead's attempted seducings. That still left his livery nag out of the noonday sun. The same could not be said for the five poor ponies baking on the sunny north side of the street near the bank. A dust-colored cuss wearing a shabby rain slicker and a drinker's nose was lounging against the hitch rail between the baking ponies

5

and the bank entrance. There wasn't a cloud in the sky and the jasper hiding his regular duds under that slicker was holding the reins of all five mounts, as if somebody might be anxious to mount up and ride in the damned near future.

Longarm knew there were imperious gents with legitimate banking business and the wherewithal to have some lesser mortal hold their horses. On the other hand, the last time he'd seen this particular setup he'd busted right into a bank robbery in progress, and the morose-looking individual out front was already staring back at him, more overtsome. Neither was out to let the other know he was staring, but Longarm was better at the game. He turned his head as if he'd noted something interesting in the window of a feed store on his side and just passed on by the firehouse and bank without so much as a casual glance their way. He could see the silly shit in that slicker just as plain, reflected in the glass on his own side of the street and, right, the ugly mutt was still watching as he decided he'd gone as far as he wanted and turned into a ladies' notion shop almost directly across from the bank.

The pretty little dishwater blonde behind the long counter of the deep but narrow notions store looked as if she suspected him of something, too, as he paused just inside her door and discovered he could cover the front entrance of the bank pretty good from right about there.

The gal behind him asked what she might do for him, adding she'd just been fixing to close for the day and go sing alto at Miss Sara Sue's wedding down at the other end of town. When Longarm said he couldn't use any ladies' notions at the moment but expected to see a robbery in progress any moment, she gasped, sobbed, and pleaded, "Take the cash in the till and dishonor me if you must, kind sir, but please don't mess up my *face,* for it's all my poor but honest parents left me when the Cheyenne run over them back in '64!"

Longarm chuckled and assured her, "Not me, here. Them, yonder. I'm the law—federal—and I suspicion the bank across the way is infested with rats. Could you work your way behind that counter and try for a peek and an educated guess on the one suspicious character in sight at the moment?"

She could and sounded a mite disappointed as she peered through the grimy glass to declare she'd never seen that saddle tramp or the scrub stock he was loitering out front with. She added, "I don't see how anyone could be planning to rob yonder bank, though. It's going on high noon and they said they'd be closing today around eleven-thirty."

Longarm thoughtfully drew his double action Colt .44-40 from its cross-draw rig under his tobacco tweed frock coat as he softly decided, "They say even Frank and Jesse know how to read, and them five ponies would be way closer to the church if anyone riding 'em in had planned on taking part in the shivaree. You don't stock guns and ammo amid all your yard goods and ribbon bows, do you, ma'am?"

She laughed incredulously but said her pals called her Penny for Penelope and that her Uncle Dan, who she minded the shop for, did keep his old army repeater in the back. When she added he'd have to ask her uncle about buying the same, Longarm explained, "I only want to borrow it for a few minutes and I swear I'll clean it and pay for any rounds I fire, if push comes to shove."

She looked hesitant. He fished out his wallet with his free hand to flash his badge her way as he insisted, "My Winchester's with my saddle and saddle bronc in the infernal firehouse. That one in the rain slicker, alone, looks to be packing something more serious than this pistol of mine, concealed. The four riding with him are apt to have me out-ranged as I attempt to dispute their departure from, oh, I'd make her about a mite over seventy-five yards."

She still looked hesitant and demanded, "What if there's nobody in yonder bank at all?"

To which he could only reply, "I won't have to clean your uncle's repeater. Since you'd know better than me, were they fixing to shoot them anvils before or after the ceremony?"

She answered, "Both. The blacksmith *likes* to shoot anvils and he'll have plenty of time. What on earth might that have to do with the bank across the way?"

He said he'd tell her if she'd fetch that infernal repeater, so, being a woman with the curiosity of her kind she ducked in the back, to return, along his side of the counter, with a Model '63 Spencer seven-shot carbine, chambered for caliber .50 rim-fire shorts, meaning an awesomely lethal amount of lead with just enough powder to back its brag out to two hundred yards. Penny smelled way better than the greasy old gun as she handed it to him. He reholstered his .44-40 and checked the tube magazine in the carbine's old stock. He could see nobody had stood inspection with this weapon since the war and, even when new, Spencer ammo had been a mite notorious. But a quick check persuaded him that Uncle Dan, Lord love him, had reloaded with fresh brass a time or two since he'd brought this old widow-maker back from the war, most likely having ridden for the Union, unless he'd robbed the dead in his salad days. Longarm didn't think it would have been polite to ask, and in any case she was pestering him about that anvil shooting. So he told her, as he reloaded the Spencer, "Bank robbers tend to rob banks the same fool ways. That's how come we got so many bank robbers in prison. I suspect they waited 'til just before the bank across the way barred its doors for the day. Then they ducked inside as the last and doubtless only customers to make a serious withdrawal."

She glanced nervously through the glass at the shabby stranger baking in the noonday sun in front of the bank, but demanded, "Why would they still be hanging about, then? I just told you that bank closed for the day a good half hour ago."

Longarm nodded and said, "They likely shut their vault, time lock and all, even earlier. That's what messed things up for the James and Younger brothers over in Northfield back in '76. Bankers just hate to get held up by the last customers of the day so they tend to put the serious cash away with the safe time-locked 'til the following business day. Over in Northfield they put a gun muzzle against the head teller's skull and told him to open or else. But he couldn't and so all they got for their trouble, even after they'd blown his brains out, was a mighty hard time, and Lord only knows how Frank and Jesse ever managed to ride out of that melee. Nobody *else* did and I doubt the boys in the bank across the way intend to repeat such a swamping mistake. I figure they figure to blow the safe, using the cover of that anvil shooting with most everyone in town gathered 'round to admire such a loud but expected bang."

She told him he had to be awfully smart to figure all that out, just from one saddle tramp and five scrub ponies doing nothing much.

He said, "I could be wrong. It happens. Meanwhile I'd sure like you to go out the back door or, failing that, at least get back behind the counter with some bales betwixt you and all that window glass."

She started to do as she was told. He admired the view of her headed the other way as well. Then the flooring beneath them and everything else for miles around tingled to the mighty roar of a one hundred-pound anvil flinging another one rooftop high in the middle distance. Then, sure enough, there came a softer thud most anyone but Longarm might have taken for a serious echo.

He cocked the Spencer and snapped, "Take cover and be quick about it, girl." Then he counted under his breath long enough to gut a bank vault and stepped out on the plank walk and away from the windows of the notions shop with Uncle Dan's Spencer politely cradled in his arms. That wasn't polite enough for the jasper across the way in the shabby slicker. He produced a Winchester Yellow Boy from under the same and Lord only knew what he might have done with it had not Longarm punched him in the chest with a .50 Short and back-flipped him over that hitch rail to land dishrag limp on the walk, holding on to neither his weapon nor the reins of all those ponies.

Thus it came to pass that as the four inside popped out en masse to see what all the fuss was about, the first thing they saw was the rumps of their getaway mounts, going every which way, as only a pony spooked by gunfire can go. Longarm downed another before they got around to noticing him. From the way one yipped as all three crawfished back inside, he made it two dead and one wounded, at least.

In the end, he turned out to have guessed optimistic. The one he'd hulled in the doorway had died soon after on the blood-slicked floor inside. The floor had been blood-slicked by the way the gang had murdered the three bank employees ahead of time, with knives, as they'd waited for the anvil shooting down the way to cover their safe-cracking. Longarm found out about all the above within the hour, when the remaining bank robbers surrendered to the considerable assemblage of town and country gun-toters attracted by the dulcet tones of Uncle Dan's repeating carbine. A constant fusillade through every window and an occasional shout about coal oil or blasting powder seemed to have a reforming effect on the outlaw mind. Longarm suspected that had he been pinned down by as many angry Apaches he'd have tried to hold out until dark, or, failing that, gone down fighting. For Apaches were no worse than a small-town mob avenging the death of three of its own, and one of 'em a nice old lady.

The poor simps who surrendered seemed to think it counted when they swore their boss, who'd died inside, had been the mean kid with a barlow knife. Longarm and, to his credit, the town law of Aurora tried to talk the boys into more formal procedures, leading in due course to the same rope dance for the both of them. But everyone who'd ever been to a public hanging knew how soon things were over when they strung the sons of bitches professional. So the townsfolk who'd known the dead bank employees, together with riders from near and far who'd come in for a swell shivaree, sent the sons of bitches off with the help of a handy cottonwood grove, slip nooses, and some more of

10

the blacksmith's blasting powder.

Longarm didn't hang around to watch. He couldn't get the town law and two deputies to back him and had to agree it would be dumb to die for anyone who stuck barlow knives in nice old ladies. But just the same it sounded disgusting to leave a man with his feet on the ground, with his hands tied behind his back, a slip noose around his neck, and a fused bomb improvised from black powder and a rubber contraceptive shoved up his ass, then lit.

The next day being the Sabbath, Longarm didn't catch hell for mixing in local vigilance committee matters in an election year until Monday morning, when his boss, U.S. Marshal William Vail of the Denver District Federal Court, lay in wait for him at the office with a copy of the *Denver Post* and some very rude wires from the Justice Department.

They were naturally back in Vail's oak-paneled inner sanctum lest they shock she-male help in the marble corridors out front or even Henry, the pallid clerk who played typewriter for them in the reception chamber. The shorter, stubbier, older, and more growlsome Billy Vail sat forted behind his cluttered desk as Longarm smoked a three-for-a-nickel cheroot in the leather guest chair on his side of the ramparts, pretending there was an ashtray some damned where around here.

Since there wasn't, he discreetly rubbed some ash into the rug for the carpet mites as he repeated his defense. Vail said, "Watch them ashes, and it don't matter who might or might not have had jurisdiction. Neither Adams County nor the Centennial State of Colorado will accept five torn-apart cadavers as a gift. Aurora's even trying to stick us with burying 'em over to Camp Weld, seeing a federal lawman gunned more than half of 'em."

Longarm started to flick more ash on the rug, decided not to, and protested, "Had the town law been minding its own beeswax I'd have never had to gun nobody. So you know they're just trying to sweep what their own boys done under the rug."

Vail grimaced and said, "It's my understanding they swept most of the results into one big ash can, mixed, and I'd be willing to go along with sinking said can in the Camp Weld garbage dump along with them dead Indians, if we wanted record-one of a federal deputy being involved in the disgusting mess."

Vail made an even meaner face at the *Denver Post* he was holding as if it was a drowned cat, adding, "It's just as well we had to send you out in the field, oh, last Thursday or Friday, let the records show. For as anyone can see, the fool papers tend to leap all over conclusions about a famous lawman like yourself."

Longarm said he'd noticed that and asked where he might have gone, after whom, already.

Vail said, "Not so fast. I know why you rid out to Aurora when I'd told you to head somewheres more sensible, you randy rascal. Henry told me about that message for you from the redhead as used to run the Aurora post office."

Longarm protested, "She lured me out yonder under false pretenses and I never, if that's what you're asking."

Vail looked relieved and said it was, adding, "Nobody *else* out yonder who could say you'd spent the night with her instead of say the Ouachita Mountains where the Indian Nation and Arkansas line gets sort of undecided?"

Longarm blinked in surprise and said, "There was a blonde less married up than any redhead but, no, I lit out soon after them bank robbers surrendered and so did a doubtless relieved bride and groom, come to study on it. I follow your drift as to why I'd best be somewhere else for the next few days, Billy. But what have we to worry about in the far-off Ouachitas?"

Vail relit his stumpy black cigar. Longarm couldn't fathom why, since that pungent brand seldom stayed lit and stunk like skunk cabbage when it did. Vail blew an evil cloud Longarm's way and explained, "We wouldn't, as a rule, and if I didn't owe Judge Isaac Parker a turn or two. He just asked for you by name, again. He seems to think you get on better with Indians and the rehashed breed of mountain whites one finds on our side of the Mississippi since the war. Opinion seems divided as to whether eastern Indians druv west against their will or hillbillies who left the Blue Ridges or Smokies owing money and wedding rings turned out more cantankersome."

Vail rummaged through the rat's nest of crumpled papers atop his desk to produce an onion skin report he needed for some facts and figures as he continued, "Seems some sneaky ridge runners, red or white, from either side of the line, have been cutting down witness trees along the official border, wherever in thunder it may be without no witness trees to say. You see, when they surveyed the line back in Old Hickory times they found it easier to draw string-straight lines on paper maps than over hill and dale in unsettled and mighty timbered hills, so . . ."

"I know what is a witness tree," Longarm cut in, adding, "We had some back in West-by-God-Virginia when I was growing up, albeit by then most folk holding clear title to taxable land preferred outcrops of bedrock, boulders too big to shift in the night, or even a post hole filled with cement and a big bronze survey stake to some big old tree blazed with a broad axe and numbered with an awl. Counting your blessings on anything mortal as a witness tree can lead to all sorts of trouble from man or nature."

Vail growled, "I just said that. Some unnatural cause has been cutting down ancient hardwoods or, even worse, blazing and numbering trees too young to have been there when the Indian Nation was surveyed close to half a century ago."

Longarm noticed his always angry-looking superior's cigar had gone out again as Vail grumbled, "It gets worse. Both the state of Arkansas and the disgruntled Choctaw Nation, whose boundary lines seem most trifled with, have demanded a new survey."

Longarm protested he'd been called a heap of things in his time but that licensed surveyor couldn't have been one of them.

Vail snapped, "Shut up and listen, then. Nobody never asked you to survey no string-straight lines or even crooked-ass ones through the Ouachitas and, to tell the truth, I was fixing to tell Judge Parker to send one of his own deputies when this shit about you in the papers changed my worried mind. Some government surveyors departed Fort Smith this very spring, to be heard from never again. A couple of deputies Judge Parker sent searching for 'em seem to have turned up missing as well. That's when certain old boys in higher places recalled you having better luck in other parts of the Indian Nation. Nobody knows whether trash whites or renegade Choctaws have been messing with them witness trees or trying to prevent new witness blazings. Nobody can figure who'd be most likely to come out ahead, or how. Few whites have settled in the Ouachitas on the Arkansas side whilst the Indians hold most of what's still hunting ground on their side in common. So who'd be most likely to come out ahead by shifting the infernal boundary line a few furlongs either way?"

Longarm started to ask a dumb question. Then he nodded soberly and decided, "Right, a few furlongs is about as far as anyone could hope to steal by murdering a witness tree or cutting down a government surveyor now and again. Meanwhile we're talking about marginal range where the timber's been cleared, or peckerwood timbering where it ain't. What about water rights?"

Vail grumbled, "How in blue blazes am I supposed to answer that from ahint this desk in Colorado? Go see for your fool self whether it's over water rights, mineral rights, or hell, some ragged-ass Indian notion. Then bring us whoever might be doing what, dead or alive."

Chapter 2

Longarm boarded the eastbound flyer with plenty of reading matter and little hope of anything more interesting to look at for the next nine hundred miles. The scenery outside was a mite tedious because so much of it was gently rolling prairie with the greenup flowers faded and the sunflowers nowheres near to opening. The scenery *inside* his sit-up coach car or the club car he preferred to sit up in was a mite tedious because it was a workday and only rich or serious folk felt up to whiling away a whole workday afternoon staring out at passing telegraph poles and sunflower sprouts.

Longarm took advantage of the nearly deserted club car to spread a schooner of beer, a bowl of filberts, and the *Rocky Mountain News* across a table he had all to himself. They'd got their pal, Crawford of the *Post*, to play down Longarm's part in the messy bank robbery and even messier end of the bank robbers. But the infernal *News* had his name all over their front page, in more than one place, as if he was famous for blowing up badmen with black powder. Neither paper had run Billy Vail's demands for a retraction, yet.

Billy didn't aim to cloud up and rain all over 'em before he was in a better position to prove his mild-mannered Deputy Long had been over in the Ouachitas for some time. Vail and Longarm both knew others would come forward to back up the reports of such a famous lawman foiling outlaws just outside the Denver City limits. What they were counting on was the simple fact that Western folk were *used* to heaps of steaming bullshit in the papers about Western gunfighters, good, bad, and mythical. That asshole Ned Buntline had published the love story of Wild Bill and Calamity Jane Cannary over the vociferous objections of the Widow Hickok, née Agnes Lake Thatcher of flying trapeze fame, and of course one could always win a bar bet by producing that penny dreadful magazine serial about Deadwood Dick, published in London with its copyrights saying flat out that no resemblance to any real persons, dead or alive, had ever been intended.

Longarm had stopped packing a copy about in a saddlebag after he'd had to pistol-whip one of the true Deadwood Dicks he'd run into in a mining camp saloon. Some drunks sure took their own bullshit serious. He saw by eyewitness accounts on the second page that Frank and Jesse had stopped a train out California way, no matter what those Pinkertons might say about survivors of the shot-up gang laying low close to their old Missouri stomping grounds of late.

In sum, those readers who still had faith in perpetual motion and magnetic baldness cures were never going to believe Billy Vail when he told little white lies, whilst those who'd been lied to so often by so many were apt to assume the fool reporters were just bullshitting some more about well-known federal deputies. Billy Vail had often said his job was more political than morally uplifting.

Longarm didn't like to lie and, had it been up to him alone, he'd have just owned up to leaving those sadistic bastards to the sadistic pleasures of the so-called vigilance committee. He'd warned the town law that even cur dogs had certain constitutional rights and the town law had warned him right back that the boys were getting restless and that local crimes were best left to local justice.

Billy Vail was likely still upset about that congressional hearing they'd had to sit through, just for angering some crooked congressmen. Meanwhile, yonder stood a muley cow atop a rise with a couple of coyote pups worrying it, and that was more interesting than any bank robber with black powder up his ass. You could worry about whether an innocent muley cow made it through the coming night alive or not.

By the time they'd left the prairie tableau behind, Longarm had decided one muley or hornless cow could hold its own against no more than a pair of overambitious coyotes. It usually took at least three wolves to pull down a grown cow, and coyotes in any numbers rarely tried. Cows and even deer could do a low-slung canine more damage with their hooves than most coyotes were willing to risk.

"Is this seat taken?" asked a she-male voice just as Longarm was getting desperate for something else to look at. So he stared up at her instead of out at all that grass and decided on the spot that a man had no right to think anyone that pretty had to be stupid just because she asked stupid questions.

He rose to his feet, hat in hand, to make room for her at the table as she graciously planted her rather ample but shapely behind in the chair that any damned fool but a beautiful woman should have seen was empty. He'd asked a damned fool question or more in his time, seeking company aboard a lonesome train.

By the time he'd gotten the *Rocky Mountain News* out of their way and resumed his own seat, they'd established that she was a Miss Magnolia Gray of the Tidewater Maryland Grays and that the drink she'd toted to their table was sarsaparilla with just a teeny weeny dash of rum in it to help her breathe better at this altitude.

He soberly agreed rum was good for delicate lungs and gave his own name as John Brown, who allowed his friends

17

to call him Jack. He could see right off she didn't believe that. He hadn't meant her to. Whether anyone had ever named her Magnolia or not, her accent was too twangy for her high-toned Tidewater airs, and though she'd removed the ring from the third finger of her left hand, its pale ghost against the slight suntan of her manicured and nicely formed hand gave her own masquerade away. The question still to be resolved was whether she was after free eats and drinks at the expense of a fellow traveler or out for true adventure.

He estimated her age between her late twenties to early thirties, given just how many other adventures she'd had up to now and allowing even a sweet young thing to have the beginnings of a double chin if she was treating boredom with sweets and rum.

She was otherwise cameo-featured with that ivory-smooth, flawless complexion that so often went with hair black as midnight and eyes blue as the Montana sky in August. Her fashionable summer-weight bodice and Dolly Varden skirts were shiny black as well. She should have had a hat pinned atop her piled-up hair, drinking in public like this, but she'd likely left that with the rest of her baggage, in a compartment, he hoped. She might have taken it as a question about her plans for the coming night, instead of concern for her belongings, if he'd asked, so he didn't ask. Despite her dumb questions about seating arrangements in a danged near-empty car, or perhaps because of them, Longarm had her down as a well-traveled gal who knew how to take care of herself and anything else she was at all interested in.

After figuring that much out, a man had to give some serious thought to his own plans for the night. Back in the good old days he'd been born too late for, to hear his elders talk, women dressed in widow's weeds had always been widows, whether they wanted to be consoled or not. But in his own time Longarm had met all sorts of adventurous gals dressed all sorts of ways and, like tobacco-brown, black was a practical color to knock around a world powered mostly by coal and steam. Dried out and powdered horse shit tended to mess up pastel duds as well.

Longarm was immune to the sort of adventuress who led a man on 'til he was all het-up, before mentioning her usual fees. His code called for avoiding flat-out self-proclaimed married women as needlessly dangerous for the fleeting pleasures of their company. Widow gals or even freethinkers who dressed practical for travel and adventure were more fun than anyone else to pick up aboard a cross-country train.

As if she'd read his mind, Magnolia glanced out at the usual rolling range to demurely ask if he knew where they were and, if so, how far they might be from Kansas City.

He glanced at a wall clock down at the far end, instead of out the window, before he decided, "We'll be whipping through Limon Junction any time now, ma'am. Doubt we'll stop to jerk water anywhere this side of Cheyenne Wells, near the Colorado-Kansas line. We're almost two full hours out of Denver, now, so I'd say you'll see K.C. around two or three in the morning, if you really want to. Ain't you staying aboard this eastbound after K.C. ma'am?"

She dimpled and said, "Please call me Magnolia, ah, Jack. They told me I have to change at Kansas City if I mean to go on to Chicago."

He frowned thoughtfully and said, "You sure do. Didn't they tell you the Burlington line runs more direct to Chicago from Denver than this here U.P. division, ah, Miss Magnolia?"

She nodded but said, "I have to make a business call in Kansas City as long as I'm on my way east. You haven't told me what business you're in, Jack."

To which he could only reply, truthfully enough as soon as one studied on it, "I travel for a Denver firm interested in timber at the moment. It's none of my beeswax why you've got to pass through either K.C. or Chicago."

That should have inspired her to tell him what she was doing on this fool train. But it didn't seem to and, since he'd already allowed it was no misfortune of his own, he

19

settled for saying, "They won't be chiming us forward to the dining car this side of five o'clock so you'd best have some of these nuts, Miss Magnolia."

She tried one filbert, washed down the mighty dry results with some of her mixed drink, and didn't seem to want any more. Longarm had to agree nuts went better with beer and, thanks to the way they'd been salted, his beer was nearly gone. So he asked if she'd like him to top off her sweeter but likely stronger drink at the nearby bar.

She said, "This dry prairie air does raise a dreadful thirst, but are you sure we can afford these outrageous railroad prices, Jack?"

He hadn't asked her to pay for their fool drinks. Before he could put his foot in it Magnolia explained, "I've my own bottle of sarsaparilla extract, along with a little bit of Jamaica in my Saratoga, up forward. I've some cheese and biscuits as well and couldn't you get them to serve us an ice bucket of that draft beer you like so much?"

He smiled uncertainly and decided, "I like compartment water with a little rum in it just fine, Miss Magnolia. But you're going to have to let me spring for both our suppers if I let you feed me all your cheese and crackers."

She said that sounded fair and rose from her seat with no further ado. He had to leap up sudden to avoid being rude to a lady. He noticed she never shilly-shallied about leading the way to her private compartment a good five cars forward. He felt awkward chasing a good-looking derriere along the aisles like so and could have killed the little kid who yelled out, "Where's that cowboy running, Momma?"

He could have killed some older commentators, as well. Then they were alone in her small but luxurious Pullman compartment and, yep, she was blushing, too. But to cover up she asked where his baggage might be and whether it might not be safer under the already made-up bunk bed she seemed to be sinking into. Her compartment was near the forward end of the car, smack over the rumbling steel wheels, so he sat down close lest she fail to hear as he

20

replied, "I got everything important lashed to my saddle up in the baggage car. Anyone willing to risk the jail time for the magazines, oranges, and such I left on my coach seat can *have* 'em, for all I care."

As he removed his hat Magnolia bent forward to get into the big old Saratoga wedged between the head of her bunk bed and the wardrobe near the sliding door. She bent mighty interesting. By the north light coming through the smoke-stained glass behind her he could tell she'd cinched her waist impossibly slender inside whalebone and silk, but she never let on how much it hurt as she propped the domed top of her Saratoga open and proceeded to pour drinks and produce a fine spread.

He'd figured she was acting fancy and calling soda crackers biscuits the way rich Americans and London Towners of all persuasions tended to. But she was splitting and cheesing real down-home white flour and butter-shortening biscuits she said she'd bought fresh from that bake shop near the Union depot back in Denver. The cheese was more mysterious. He'd never been in the high-toned Denver grocery she said she'd found it in. It was soft as butter on a warm day and smelled like socks overdo for a changing. But it tasted good enough, and he hadn't known how hungry he'd gotten since those pickled pigs knuckles and boiled eggs at the Parthenon Saloon that morning.

He didn't like her notions of liquid refreshments as much. The rum was all right, but sarsaparilla always reminded him of a sick bay. It was supposed to be good for the ague as well as soda fountain sipping. He swallowed a heap to get it out of the way and then rose to refill the glass tumbler two-thirds of the way with tepid branch water from the tap above her bitty corner sink. Had he been in there alone he might have tipped up the mahogany cover of the compartment commode whilst he was at it. But he didn't know her that well, yet, and didn't really have to pee that bad to begin with.

As he sat back down she handed him another cheese-stuffed biscuit and asked if he'd like more rum with his water. He could see by the amused look in her big blue eyes why she hadn't suggested any more fool sarsaparilla. He smiled back at her and said it seemed just right for sipping, now. He resisted the impulse to mention the last time a traveling gal in a private compartment had tried to press something even more disgusting than sarsaparilla on him. He was pretty sure this one had no reason to spike his drink with chloral hydrate. She didn't know who he was and he'd told her flat out he was traveling by coach car. The hire of this private compartment cost more than his ready-made suit was worth and he could see by her own outfit that Magnolia knew clothes and what they might cost.

They rode on a time in awkward, chewing silence, each knowing what the other was thinking but not wanting to trip over their own feet as the band played on. He could tell, and he knew she could tell he could tell, she'd waltzed to this refrain before, doubtless more than once.

That seemed only fair. He'd have never followed her all the way here had he wanted to read every one of those fool magazines or drink himself stupid back yonder. He knew Queen Victoria wouldn't be amused and he'd gotten in trouble this way before. But as he was hoping this particular stranger on a train would agree, nothing made time pass quicker, traveling far and wide, than the uncertainties of sweet romance. For as everyone knew who'd ever loved and lost, you just never knew how much time you had to work with, or if it would be enough, and hence he caught her glancing out at the passing prairie from time to time, not at the drab grassy rises, but to see just how that old sun ball was doing as it slid down the west slope of the early summer sky. He knew what she was thinking. It would have been coltish to say they'd best get on with it if they meant to get her out of that fool corset and back into it by Kansas City. So he settled for saying, "Lord have mercy if I ain't too stuffed right now for any sit-down supper up forward."

When she agreed but said she'd had no idea of the time, he soothed, "We can always have some sandwiches sent back if we get hungry, later. Having to worry about getting off at such an awkward hour sure makes it tough to plan one's *earlier* evening. I mean if either of us was just traveling on through K.C. in times more suited to early-rising milkmen there'd be no problem. We could just go on snoring as they switched this car to the Saint Lou tracks and . . ."

"Why, Mr. Brown, whatever are you suggesting?" She cut in archly, batting her big blue eyes at him as they both tried not to laugh. He returned her innocent gaze with a skill honed at many a poker table and replied, "I never said whether you'd want to be snoring alone or not by the time we'll likely part forever, either way, Miss Magnolia. I leave such choices for the lady. I was riz to treat ladies with respect, *or decent,* leastways."

For some reason that made her laugh. Then she said it would be jake with her if he wanted to hang up his coat but not to get any disrespectful ideas. So he assured her he wouldn't and, yep, they'd both been through all this bull before. The art of seduction, from a man's point of view, consisted of simply letting the innocent young things seduce him and not saying or doing anything dumb enough to change their skittish she-male minds. Longarm had long since learned there was nothing a man could do, short of physical force, when or if a gal simply didn't want him. On the other hand, once a gal *did,* and he didn't mess up, there was little he had to remember but the simple facts of life, with most gals preferring to start on the bottom.

He hung his gun rig on the same wall hook as long as he was at it. He always had the double derringer in his vest pocket if he was dead wrong about her feelings for him. As he sat back down the train seemed to be slowing. When she commented on that he glanced out again, shook his head, and said, "Just coming to a trestle. I told you we wouldn't stop this side of Cheyenne Wells."

She asked when that might be. He thought and decided, "This side of sundown at the rate we're going. Last time I caught this run out of Denver I was just sitting down

23

to supper, forward, when some hungry-looking breed kids spoiled my appetite by rubbing their bitty noses all over the outside of the dining car window. They got a couple of half-Cheyenne families left in Cheyenne Wells and it takes nigh five full minutes to jerk water and swap mailbags there."

Magnolia grimaced and suggested that in that case he might like to pull down the blinds. He did. There were only two. The results were sort of dark in there. He started to say something really dumb about the lamp fixture over the sink. He'd already told her he believed in Lady's Choice and it was up to her if she wanted to break the spell with the harsh realities of lamplight.

She didn't seem to. She giggled and said this reminded her of crawling under the house with her cousins, back home in the Tidewater. He didn't ask whether her cousins had been male or she-male. He knew kids playing under the house could get pretty silly, either way. He'd used the exercise with the stiff, balky blinds as an excuse to sit a mite closer. He could tell by the way she was breathing that she'd noticed. He knew anything he might say might cross her legs so he didn't say anything. She shut the top of her Saratoga, as if clearing the decks for action, as she demurely asked whether his own baggage, like some of her own, had been booked through to Chicago or on to Saint Lou. He figured she was trying to figure the time they had left to get down to brass tacks, too. He wasn't thinking of anything sneakier when he casually replied he was bound for neither destination she'd mentioned. He said, "I have to go down around Fort Smith for my, ah, firm. You can only get there dog-legging through K.C. because there ain't a more direct line through the Indian Nation, yet."

The temperature in the hitherto cozy compartment seemed to drop a good ten degrees, even though all she said was oh, in a tone that would have made a brass monkey shiver.

He'd messed up. He couldn't see how, but like every man born of mortal woman, he'd messed up before, he'd likely

24

mess up again, and he knew the feeling all too well.

He didn't ask her what he'd said wrong. He knew he'd just admitted to being bound for Fort Smith and it was up to her to tell him why she'd apparently equated that with an admission he was married, to his ugly sister, and had a loathsome social disease as well.

She took her own sweet time and even then she went on asking instead of answering. He could have lied some more, of course, but since she really seemed upset at any man headed for Fort Smith he decided it couldn't hurt to assure her, "I'm only passing through Fort Smith on my way to the Ouachita Mountains, a fair piece south. Lest you take me for one of them sinister youths Fort Smith is so famous for hanging, I'd best admit I'm a lawman, riding for Uncle Sam, and I doubt I could be after anyone you might know in them parts, Miss Magnolia."

She gasped, "I should think no! I told you where I was from and where I'm going, as the owner of a good block of mining stock, thank you very much!"

He chuckled and told her, "You don't have to thank me for your mining stock, Miss Magnolia. I already told you I was headed south of Fort Smith to study trees. But since this seems to have upset you I'll just be on my way and we'll say no more about it."

He started to rise. She grabbed his thigh, digging her nails through his tweed like a kitten playing rough as she demanded, "What are *you* upset about, Jack? That is your name, isn't it?"

He smiled sheepishly and allowed, "As much as your name might be Magnolia, ma'am. You'll note I never asked why you were so upset. It's no never mind of mine who's waiting for you in Fort Smith or why you wanted me to recall you as a lady bound for Chicago once we'd parted friendly in K.C. Since no damage has been done and I can get off the far end of a train mighty discreet, why don't we just drop the subject here and now?"

She sighed and said, "If only. All right, I am a recent widow and there *is* someone waiting for me in Fort Smith to do something about that. I don't know whether I want him to or not. I wasn't fibbing about the stock portfolio my late husband left me and a girl can't be too careful about sweet-talking fortune hunters."

Longarm leaned back a mite more relaxed to assure her most men would admire her whether she had a stock portfolio or not.

She heaved a sad little sigh and said, "I'm over thirty and starting to put on weight. I've just never been able to control my appetite for food and other carnal pleasures. Some say my late husband might have lived a little longer had I fed him and . . . you know, with less vigor. Be that as it may, I'm a woman with strong feelings and I have to be in firm control when I join Clarence in Arkansas. You see, we'll be on another train together for two whole days and nights and I've already told you he's asked me to marry him."

Longarm shot her a puzzled frown and asked, "What's got you all het-up about your strong feelings, then? No offense, but I don't think you ought to wed old Clarence if the thought of feeling strong with him unsettles you."

She insisted, "That's just the point. How would I ever get out of it when the two of us arrive back east after, you know?"

He nodded and said, "In sum, you'd like to meet up with him in Fort Smith cool and collected. Is that why you picked me up a night early, ma'am?"

She grimaced and said, "I wish you wouldn't put it that way. You make me sound so low. I'm not sure just what I wanted from you on my way to meet Clarence. Maybe I just wanted to flirt a little to sort of get back in practice. Maybe I wanted more. It's been almost a year since I've done anything with any man and, oh, Jack, I'm all mixed-up and you'll have to tell me what's best for me!"

Longarm sighed and said, "All right. For openers I'd best go on back to the club car and sup on nuts and pretzels.

Then you and your Clarence work things out as best you can for, like I said, I'll be getting off another car and . . ."

"Don't you *want* me? Have I really gotten *that* fat?" she cut in.

To which he could only truthfully reply, "I want you so bad I can taste it. But you never asked me that. You asked me what would be the best for you. I have met me a gal or two on cross-country trains, Miss Magnolia. I may have met one on this very car, for all I know, and in any case the scene is ever different but ever a mite the same. So I may have a better picture than you of the miles ahead betwixt here and Fort Smith."

"You think I'm a fat silly." She pouted.

He patted her skirted thigh—there was a mite more of her down there than expected—and soothed, "You know you're a head-turning belle if you've been paying any mind to men at all. We both know I could reel you in for some slap and tickle and we'd have a grand old time most of the way to K.C."

He sighed and added, "Then we'd have to get dressed again, change to that southbound in the cold gray dawn of reality, and ride all the way to Clarence by harsh, accusing sunlight."

She quietly asked, "Couldn't we keep the blinds down and avoid harsh accusations at least until Van Buren? My KC&S timetable says we won't have to worry about Clarence before high noon. We'll have that four-hour layover in Kansas City in any case and if you'd like to catch a later train . . ."

So he muttered, "Well, I tried," and reeled her in for some of that slap and tickle they'd both been anxious to get down to. From the French accent of her hungry, wet kisses she'd been even more anxious. But she'd said she hadn't been with a man, this way, for close to a year, and from the speed with which she shucked everything but her black lace corset, silk stockings and high-button shoes, she'd been celibate too long to endure another damned moment.

He did his best to soothe her feelings by entering her with his undershirt still in place and his fool pants still around his booted ankles. From the way she hugged his bare hips with her ample creamy thighs and hugged him to her heroic marshmallow breasts she was mighty grateful. She came ahead of him, more than once, and begged him to strip down all the way and let her kiss him all over. He came in her, hard, before he felt relaxed enough to let her have her wicked way with him.

Magnolia, if that was her name, was acting wicked indeed when the train stopped to jerk water at Cheyenne Wells. He was glad he'd pulled the blinds. There was still a little light outside and he'd have hated to have breed kids laughing at him in such an awkward position.

They rolled on and, after sundown, Magnolia wanted him to ride the Union Pacific and her with the blinds up and the moonlit prairie reflecting romantic silvery light on their passion-flushed flesh. He kept asking her to let him uncinch that scratchy lace corset to rub bare bellies with her. But she said she was self-conscious about her dumpy figure. That's how she described it while he threw it to her dog style, admiring her broad but well-formed rump below the impossible waistline she insisted on, courtesy of modern science and the whaling industry. She hour-glassed even nicer on her back and, despite the lard even an admirer had to allow she was packing betwixt ankle and crotch these days, she could really get her well-rounded legs into some amazing positions. She'd intimated she might have endangered her late husband's health with her enthusiasm for horizontal acrobatics. But it sure seemed a swell way to kill an otherwise tedious train ride and Longarm was young, healthy, and not bad at horizontal acrobatics in his own right.

He was usually more thoughtful of his partner's literally tender feelings, but old Magnolia couldn't seem to get enough, deep as a man could get it, and so he was able to really ride to glory with her and she laughed like a

28

mean little kid when he groaned, "Powder River and let her buck!" with his puckered balls against her wet chin. It damned near gagged her to death to laugh at a time like that. But she recovered by swallowing deeper and that came close to killing *him*.

But, of course, nobody could have continued that passionately all the way across the state of Kansas. So well before Salina they'd wound up sharing a naked smoke side by side on the narrow bunk and of course it wasn't much longer before he commenced to feel her tears slopping his bare chest.

He never asked why. Women were just like that. A man could get more sensible answers asking a Pawnee star singer why he was shaking that fool rattle. Longarm took a long, thoughtful drag on his cheroot, patted her big bare ass with the other hand, and soothed, "We got a heap of time to consider the ways of getting off discreet in K.C., kitten. To begin with, the platform will be mighty murksome at that hour and we won't be the only passengers getting off."

She snuggled closer and began to toy with his limp manhood as she praised his sensitive soul. When she asked about the awkward layover in the K.C. depot, he said, "You know I'd rather meet you at a hotel Clarence might not know about, some distance from the depot and any others bound for Fort Smith. But to tell the truth my boss might worry if I don't wire him where I am about the time he expects me to be there."

She sighed and allowed she'd already wired Clarence when he might expect her to make Fort Smith. So Longarm suggested, "There's a ladies-only waiting room along with bathing facilities, coffee shops, and such if you'd like to meet me aboard the southbound, after it clears the K.C. yards."

She said she'd like that a lot and began to stroke his semierection to full attention. When she rose on her hands and knees to kiss it as well he got rid of his cheroot and insisted on doing it right, pleased with her for being such a sensible as well as sex-starved gal. But while they screwed right through Salinas he was fully dressed and lounging in his green plush coach seat as the train rolled into K.C. at a really dreadful hour of the morning.

He didn't see Magnolia or even his McClellan and Winchester as he killed a good part of the awkward layover eating waffles, drinking black coffee, and flirting with the buck-toothed but nicely built counter gal in the all-night coffee shop. The coffee woke him up a mite and the completely different build of the buck-toothed blonde restored his interest in her gender a mite, albeit in truth by now he felt more in need of sleep than sex.

They'd told him the southbound would be made up more than an hour before it left for Texarkana by way of Fort Smith. Magnolia had told him she'd have the same compartment number. So after he'd restored the confidence of that buck-toothed counter gal as much as she likely deserved, he made his way out to the platforms, yawning like a catfish at low water, and found they'd sure enough commenced to put the southbound KC&S together for that morning run.

So he got aboard, found a porter, and flashed both his tickets and courtesy pass from a more famous railroad as he asked the way to compartment M-3.

It was just as well there was no compartment M-3 aboard this particular train. Lord knew how a sleepy lawman might ever explain busting in on total strangers by the dawn's early light. As it was, in his sleepy condition, it took Longarm longer than usual to figure Magnolia had told him some big fibs.

Why a gal seeking sexual adventures might not want anyone who really knew her to know about them was less a mystery. So Longarm just laughed and settled down in a coach seat, marveling, "Clarence sounded like an asshole, too, you asshole. But what the hell, it ain't as if she didn't give you a swell time along with all them big, fat fibs."

Chapter 3

There was a small brass band and a good-sized crowd waiting on the sun-baked platform when Longarm's train rolled into Fort Smith. Nobody there seemed to have been waiting for Magnolia Gray, or even him. Some otherwise uninteresting old fart getting off in rumpled but expensive civilian duds appeared to have been a hero of the fondly remembered War Between the States. It was tougher to tell which side he'd been so brave for. Now that President Hayes had officially ended Reconstruction, you saw vets in blue and gray swapping lies and buying drinks for one another in parts where opinion had been a mite divided. Arkansas had sent twenty-five infantry regiments, ten cavalry regiments, and three artillery battalions to fight for the South while the North had recruited eight infantry regiments, half of them colored, four all-white cavalry regiments, and a battalion of artillery with way more ammunition and almost as many field pieces as the three rebel redleg battalions combined. From the way the survivors were carrying on that afternoon, a heap of fun had been had by all. A sign held by a perky young gal too young to even remember the war all that much, despite her gray kepi and reb tunic, announced all this fuss was intended to commemorate something awful the red-blooded white boys of Sebastian County had done, in concert, to some long extinct Indians.

That hardly seemed fair to Longarm. Neither the Caddo-speaking Wichita nor the Siouan but mild-mannered Quapaw who'd been out this way to begin with had menaced anyone worth mention, while the civilized tribes just across the state line to the west had fought for both sides, if mostly for the South, the same as everyone else in these parts.

But since nobody had asked Longarm to make a speech, he moseyed on to the baggage shed to reclaim his saddle and such. Then, bracing the load on his right hip, leaving his cross-draw holster free, he headed for the federal courthouse presided over by old Isaac Parker to see what the judge might have to say about those witness trees.

It was a longer trudge than it might have felt under a cooler sky with a lighter tote. But he was able to work most of the way in shade until, spying the sort of plantation house pillars and high veranda of the courthouse across the way, he picked up the pace to cross the sunny stretch faster.

Later, he'd figure that had likely been the reason the rascal laying for him with a buffalo rifle, a Sharps Big Fifty from the sound of it, missed him total in broad-ass daylight.

Longarm naturally let go his McClellan to grab for his sixgun as he crabbed sideways, cussing at the dirty linen gunsmoke rising up a darker slot betwixt two buildings across the way. He lobbed two rounds of his own that way, hoping neither would carry far enough in the middle of town to hurt anybody innocent. Then he was hunkered down behind a watering trough and nobody seemed interested in gunning him or his pile of possibles lying lonesome out yonder in the dust.

The vicinity filled with company before the last of that mysterious gunsmoke had drifted completely away. One officious asshole with a brass county badge might have given him a tougher time had not another federal deputy from across the way yelled, "Put that hog leg away before you get hurt, junior. The hombre you're threatening with it happens to be the one and original Longarm, riding with us."

That inspired a certain amount of awed respect. So Longarm was gracious enough to fill his fellow lawmen in, including local piss ants, as he reloaded and strode over to retrieve his belongings.

In turn he was told Judge Parker and Billy Vail's opposite in Fort Smith (if the Denver district marshal had taken half as much from any judge) had been called over to Little Rock to answer yet more charges of arbitrary justice. That was what sob-sister writing in Eastern papers called hanging mad dog killers—arbitrary justice. Longarm had always found the notorious hanging judge of Fort Smith firm but fair with accused crooks, and a mite stiff but downright decent to the law-abiding. The higher courts tended to set aside more than half the death sentences Old Isaac handed down, even though to date nobody had ever been able to show his court had ever wrongly convicted a soul of farting in mixed company.

The helpful Fort Smith deputy didn't know anything about the case Longarm was on, either, albeit even the county law agreed some son of a bitch with a big fifty must not have wanted him there. The federal man said Judge Parker had left Prince Maledon in charge. So Longarm said that's who he'd best see next.

Leaving his saddle and such on the plank floor of the courthouse hallway, Longarm caught up with Prince Maledon in a tack room, working up yet another hangman's noose, or halter, as professional hangmen seemed to prefer.

The cadaverous Prince of Hangmen (his parents had sprinkled him as George) stared up at Longarm friendly enough with his deep-set eyes. The effect was still sort of spooky. The Prince of Hangmen looked the part, even though he was a sort of kindly old cuss when one studied on all the things that could go wrong with a hanging.

Maledon never bungled. He prided himself on displaying neither mercy nor cruelty to his criminal clients. He could get a mite smug and insufferable when wound up about the grand occasion he'd sent Dan Evans, Bill Whittington, Jim Moore, Ed Campbell, Sam Fooy, and Smokey Mankiller to the great beyond on the same gallows in the same instant. He said he'd been tempted to let Smokey Mankiller, a really bad Cherokee, amuse the crowd with some rope dancing. But in the end his professionalism had prevailed and now even bad Cherokee asked for Prince Maledon's services if they really had to go that way.

Maledon's head hair was still dark. His full beard was snow-white. The face between looked like old Prince had been mummified one time in Egypt Land. He seemed to be smiling—it was hard to tell—as he said, "We've been expecting you, Deputy Long. I hope you understand the rules of this federal district as they apply to bringing the poor sinners in alive for a proper trial and execution?"

Longarm did. Judge Parker made his deputies pay for proper burials out of their own pockets when they gunned an owlhoot rider in the field and spoiled his fun. He smiled thinly down at Prince Maledon and said, "I never gun anyone I don't have to. I never fuck around with anyone who seems out to gun me, neither."

Maledon chuckled, a ghastly sound, the way he did it, and said they had a lot in common, rising to his full skinny height as he added, "I've gunned four I couldn't get at with my halter, so far. You'll want two good ponies for riding and packing, of course. Come on out back and take your pick from our remuda."

Longarm didn't ask why the older man was strapping on that brace of sixguns, cross-draw, as they stepped out in the hallway together. He said he'd left his saddle and such near the front door. As the grim but courteous head hangman tagged after him he added, "I wasn't planning on just mounting up and riding down to the Ouachitas on my

34

own to sniff trees. My home office didn't give me much on paper to work with."

Maledon said, "We can let you have a carbon of the charges against person or persons unknown but likely white entered by the council of the Choctaw Nation with the approval of their resident agent and the B.I.A. Some kith and kin of our own boys who vanished Lord-knows-where in the Ouachitas have been politely asked to stay out of it by Judge Parker. As your own boss likely told you, you've a rep for working spooky cases with Indian overtones. How come you get along so well with Indians, Deputy Long? No offense, but despite your tan, your eyes are too gun muzzle gray and you sport too much face hair to have much Indian blood."

Longarm shrugged and said, "Just lucky, I reckon. I get along fair with Mexicans and colored folk as well. I begin by avoiding words like *greaser* or *nigger*. Lots of trouble betwixt our kind and others seem the result of well-meant stupidity. I'd be the first to confess I don't know much about Choctaw. I've spent more time in your Cherokee and Osage strips north of the Arkansas. They're more closely akin to Creek, right?"

The Prince of Hangmen grimaced, not a pretty sight, and warned, "The Western Creek prefer Muskogee and we tell our Fort Smith deputies not to ask Choctaw or Chickasaw how they might or might not be related to other Creek speakers. Like the Cherokee, the Choctaw and Chickasaw were living white, fair-prosperous, and farming with slave labor when Andrew Jackson declared them too savage to dwell among other Southern planters. So they share the common distaste of other slavocrats for the Muskogee and Seminole."

Longarm nodded soberly and said he recalled how the Black Warrior River back in the Alabama Creek Country got its name. Maledon opined, "I doubt Muskogee or even Seminole have all that much African in them. It's just a simple fact that they took in runaway darkies instead of killing or selling them back to whites they hated worse. But what are we fussing about, son? There can't be all that many colored folk mixed up in the mystery of the witness trees on either side of the border line. Neither Choctaw nor the peckerwood ridge runners you might run into in the Ouachitas admire colored neighbors and we've already established it ain't too safe down yonder for armed *white* boys!"

A young cuss looking just a mite sissy despite his faded jeans, hickory shirt, Texas sombrero, and low-slung Remington .44 seemed to be hovering over the old McClellan Longarm had left against the baseboard near the front entrance. Before Longarm could warn the squirt to leave his stuff alone it piped up, girlishly, "I'm looking for a Deputy Long that Judge Parker said we'd have riding with us. They told me out front he was in here, somewheres."

Longarm frowned down uncertainly at the bitty stranger, too pretty to be a boy and a mite too rough around the edges to pass for a girl as he replied, "I'd be Custis Long and before you tell us who you might be, would you mind if I asked you something mighty personal?"

The young stranger blushed a tad rosier and replied, "I'd be Fiona Coyne and I dress like a boy so I can ride astride through country rough as it may be getting and, yes, I'm Irish or second generation Irish if you'd like to make anything of that. I was born in Saint Lou to parents who fled the Great Hunger from Connemara and now that that's behind us I'm Assistant Surveyor, wrangler, and camp cook to Himself, Captain Paddy Boyle of the U.S. Survey Service."

Prince Maledon murmured, "Boyle would be the gent Judge Parker would like you to keep an eye on as he runs a new beeline defining red and white hunting and grazing rights. Nobody said anything about his segundo being she-male, though."

Fiona Coyne's dark eyes blazed brightly enough for them to make out their true blue depths as she snapped, "I'll not

36

be called dirty names, even by my elders, good sir!"

Longarm soothed, "Segundo means second-in-command out our way, Miss Fiona. Old Prince here gets to hang lots of Mexicans. You coming to find me saves me looking for you and your boss."

He bent to pick up his McClellan, adding, "I was just about to find a pony out back to cinch this saddle aboard. Why don't you tell us what you and Captain Boyle are riding, and where you're camped, as I tend my chores?"

The boyish Fiona tagged along with Longarm and the Prince of hangmen willingly enough. She sounded sort of lost puppy, in fact, as she told them, going down the back steps, she'd been looking all over for her boss that morning as well. By the time Prince Maledon had led them as far as the federal remuda, housed in a rambling stable facing a dusty corral no ponies were dumb enough to bake in at the moment, they'd established that Fiona and her Captain Boyle had been staying in adjoining rooms at a nearby hotel, awaiting Longarm and apparently someone else Boyle had sent for. His pretty young assistant said she'd had no idea who, or why. When they'd said goodnight, about the time Longarm had been sharing that first smoke on the train with old Magnolia, Boyle had promised to buy them both a grand breakfast in the hotel dining room. But he'd never come down to breakfast and when, at last, she'd gone up to see why, she'd found his door unlocked and his room empty, baggage and all. She said that was all she knew and agreed it seemed awfully odd.

Prince Maledon whistled softly and muttered, "I'd say this was more than odd. Now they're vanishing on the trail before they can even get out of town!"

Chapter 4

Longarm figured an older federal employee who hung men for a living could be trusted not to play kid games with ponies. So he went along with Prince Maledon's suggestion to take the steady-looking bay barb and shorter limbed but spunky rumped paint, chestnut and white and Osage bred. Osage, being sort of sensible but recent high plains huntsmen, knew almost as much as Cayuse when it came to horse flesh, and the paint had been rebusted to accept more civilized gear and left-side mounting, Prince said.

Fiona had walked over from the hotel in her anxiety. So Longarm let her try out the paint, bareback as well as astride, while he rode the bay with his old army saddle and his cocked Winchester across his thighs.

The Indian pony didn't give the gal a hard time and nobody pegged any buffalo rounds their way as they trotted the short distance to the Riverview Hotel, which might have been more true before they'd let all those crack willows and cottonwoods spring up out back.

Captain Boyle was still missing, bag and baggage,

although his own ponies were still in the hotel stable and nobody had messed with the saddles, surveying instruments, or camping gear in the tack room when Longarm suggested Fiona look.

She proved how green she was about hotel reservations during some sort of veterans' reunion by having surrendered Boyle's room to the management without a fight. Longarm would have fought them if he hadn't felt sorry for the innocent older couple the snippy desk clerk had already hired Boyle's vacated room to. When Longarm mentioned the fee Fiona said her boss had paid in advance, the clerk snipped he didn't know anything about that. So Longarm kicked over a spittoon and threatened a lobby rubber plant with bodily harm until, sure enough, they *did* seem to have a refund coming.

Longarm told Fiona to hang on to it. She'd already said Friday was payday, whether her blamed boss got back in time or not.

Leaving their livestock and trail possibles in the care of a more sensible young stablehand, then locking the one room left and pocketing the key, Longarm led the way to the nearby Western Union, explaining along the way that gents who vanished with no sign of a struggle often left voluntary. Fiona agreed an urgent wire delivered in the wee small hours might have done it. She looked away as she quietly confided Captain Boyle had tried to enter her bedchamber after dark on one occasion and promised never to try that again.

Longarm was paid to be nosey and he knew men had vanished from the face of the earth for less, so as they approached the black and yellow sign of the telegraph office he urged her to run that past him slower in more detail.

She blushed becomingly and murmured, "*A mo mala* and it was only the usual door bumps and blather of a man with too much to drink and no woman willing to comfort him. I told you he only tried it once and that was days ago when we met in Little Rock and he discovered I was a girl for all my degrees in geometry, geography, and botany, and all and all."

"I was a mite surprised to meet you just now, my ownself," Longarm mused, half to himself, before asking, "How much of a drinking problem are we talking about, and remember you're answering a federal lawman, not a neighbor lady over a fence."

She shook her head and said, "I'd not call Himself a drunk. Captain Boyle's a retired army engineer with a good reputation in our game."

"How well might you know your game?" He insisted.

To which she replied as insistently, "Better than yourself and no doubt many another in pants, thank you very much. I told you I held trade school degrees, and it was in the footsteps of a favorite uncle and older brother I put myself through all those courses."

Her voice got way smaller as they entered the telegraph office. A man with less keen hearing might not have heard her say she'd signed up after her brother and favorite uncle had been arrowed in the Black Hills by Lakota. He didn't ask why. Senator Hearst was still hauling high-grade out of those hills and the deadwood mines hadn't bottomed yet, either.

They bellied side by side to the counter inside. Longarm flashed his badge and ID at the young telegraph clerk and, wouldn't you know it, she was pretty and inclined to smile back, too.

So they didn't have the usual fuss about the privacy of messages sent to or by others for a nickel a word. The brown-headed Western Union gal dug right into her files when he explained it was urgent, as if she believed him. She said they'd sent close to a dozen telegrams by messenger boy to the Riverview the night before. But after that she was way less help. She had nothing on anyone named Boyle sending or receiving message-one. Longarm pressed her to make sure. She offered to let him go through the file drawer himself, explaining, "The client writes the message on one

40

of those company blanks you see down by the inkwells at the end of this very counter. We can't send that anywhere by electricity. We send the message letter for letter in dots and dashes and the writing stays right here, to be filed for future conversations like the one we seem to be having."

Fiona insisted, "Himself has sent many a telegram from Fort Smith in the few short days we've been here. It was hardly my place to read any but he told me himself he'd wired his home office and his family in Virginia City where we were staying, when we might be leaving and all and all."

Longarm started to ask which Virginia City they were talking about. He didn't see why he wanted to know, just yet. So he soothingly said, "They only hold on to telegraph blanks a day or so, Miss Fiona."

The pretty clerk nodded and chipped in, "Less, if this veterans' reunion keeps up. I swear I didn't know either side had half that many men and it's a wonder they didn't both lose, as foolish as some of the wires the old fools keep sending!"

It was Longarm's turn to look away lest his feelings show. He supposed that to gals now in their early twenties his introduction to manhood at Shiloh did rank somewhere with the Norman Conquest, if not the discovery of fire. But he wasn't ready to feel like an old fool yet. He wasn't more than eight or ten years older than either of them, blast their flat chests, pigtails, and doubtless bratty behavior whilst he and like-minded teenagers had been learning to shoot and salute.

Thanking the snip behind the counter, Longarm led Fiona back outside and thence, since the streets seemed crowded despite the afternoon heat, to an out-of-the-way beanery only Fort Smith residents or gents who'd been through more than once might know about.

A trio of old soldiers, one in blue and two in butternut gray, had already grabbed one of the three bitty booths. Longarm led Fiona to another. She allowed the place smelled funny.

41

He told her he just didn't know of any Fort Smith beanery serving boiled spuds and cabbage, and when one of the breed sisters who ran the place came out from the back to take their order he told Fiona to trust him and ordered them the specialty of the house, Bible Cake and Cherokee coffee.

Fiona said she'd never tried Cherokee cuisine before. He told her, "Sure you have, if you've ever et far south as Saint Lou. The Cherokee had almost forgot they were Indians when land grabbers east of the Big River discovered how savage they were and got Andy Jackson and Winfield Scott to herd 'em out this way. They were sort of stray Iroquois who'd been farming for generations along the Tennessee when our kind caught up with 'em. They had tobacco, deer skins, and freshwater pearls to sell, so the traders were anxious to expose them to the notions of Civilization and they took to it like ducks take to water. That's how come they're listed as one of the civilized tribes."

The plump but not bad-looking sister brought their order on a tray, put it down, and left before anyone could say anything she was supposed to get sore about. She was at least half white and hence knew better than some how white folk could sound mean when they were only trying to sound amusing.

The Irish-American girl across from him sniffed suspiciously at her coffee mug and asked, "Does this have what I think it has in it?"

He nodded and said, "I doubt it's bonded but I don't work for the pesky Treasury Department and they've yet to poison anyone with a few drops of corn squeezings in that genuine Arbuckle Brand coffee. Like I said, ducks to water, and if you want to split hairs, coffee is an Arabian notion we have no more right to than your average Indian."

Fiona dimpled and said, "Nobody said a bit of poteen in good coffee was a crime against nature, and who'd be paying for revenue stamps when the money could be better spent on more malt? Why do they call this Bible Cake? It looks like plain pound cake to me."

He said, "Eat some, then. I ain't a baker but the way I hear tell they call that breed of baking a Bible Cake because they make it out of stuff from the Good Book."

He saw she didn't follow his drift, likely being an Irish bapist who didn't get to read the Good Book in English and hence felt less inclined to quote from it than some country folk.

He thought and said, sort of solemn, " 'And all they of the land came to a wood and there was *honey* upon the ground.' Samuel 14:25. 'As the partridge sitteth upon *eggs* and hatcheth them not.' Jeremiah 17:11. 'Or all thy strongholds shall be as fig trees with the first ripe *figs*.' From Nahum 3:12. Taste the figs? I think the raisins come from Samuel, too, and of course the sweet cane sugar's from Jeremiah where they got them eggs."

Fiona laughed and said, "I think the spices in great abundance must be from Chronicles and if not this is still grand cake to go with such voluptuous coffee. But are your darling Cherokee such Bible-thumping Christians and all and all?"

He nodded soberly and said, "Mostly fundamentalists. You'll find more Roman Catholics among the Nadene or Apache and your so-called Sioux or Lakota."

She blinked in surprise and protested, "That can't be true! Everyone knows those savages who killed my poor brother, Uncle Sean, and even General Custer pray to heathen gods and all and all!"

He gave himself a mental kick for having reminded the poor gal of morose matters. But now the fat was in the fire. So he said, "I doubt many folk of any complexion worry about their professed faith while they're robbing and killing one another. Indians can sound as dumb as us about such matters. Depending on the axe one has to grind one can pontificate about grinding said axe for love of Saint Mary or Spider Woman, who drew this world up from the depths for her red children alone, and who said anything about that including Paiutes who ought to go back where they came from."

She laughed and confided her parents had never had much use for those shiftless Kerry men when employment was hard to find and all and all. She washed down more Bible Cake and asked what he could tell her about the Indians they'd be meeting down in the Ouachita Mountains.

He grimaced and confided, "I could tell you more about the Utes and Arapaho out Denver way, or these Cherokee I've worked around before. But since the Choctaw are considered one of the civilized tribes, and since we ain't supposed to meet all that many . . ."

"Why not?" she cut in. "And wasn't it the Choctaw themselves who demanded a new survey of their boundary lines?"

He nodded and said, "They did and that's why I don't expect to have much trouble with 'em or even meet all that many, Miss Fiona."

He sipped some coffee, himself, and continued, "Folk fiddling with boundary lines have little call to demand a fresh government survey. But why am I telling a government surveyor this? You'd know better than me just who might have been doing what, with what, to whom down along the eastern verge of the Indian Nation, right?"

She protested she didn't know beans, explaining her missing boss, Captain Boyle, was the one in charge of their intended expedition.

He smiled thinly and replied, "No, he ain't. He ain't here. Unless he gets back from wherever he's gone, *poco tiempo,* I'd say *you're* the one the Choctaw Nation, the state of Arkansas, and Uncle Sam's depending on to put things to right down yonder, Miss Fiona."

She stared thundergasted across the table at him, protesting, "You can't be serious! I don't even know what the problem is and all and all!"

He shrugged and insisted, "We'll give Boyle once around the clock to either get himself back on the job or at least get in touch with you, me, the survey service, or at least his fool family. If he's still among the completely missing

44

by this time, tomorrow, we'd best plan on riding on down to find out for ourselves what the problem might be."

He sipped more spiked coffee. They'd made it a mite strong for this early a start. She said, "I don't dare leave town with all that expensive government equipment unless someone authorizes me to go on with the survey in Captain Boyle's place."

Longarm nodded and said, "Let me worry about that. I'm good at sending wires. It's all in how you pose the suggestions. We'll want to leave town discreet, after dark, lest *we* wind up vanishing too."

She repressed a shudder and murmured, "That's right. Someone seems to be after *you* as well. What if they spot us leaving? Won't they be able to figure out we've left, in any case, once we have?"

He nodded grimly and said, "I'm better at covering such bets out in open country than in a crowdsome town with all sorts of hidey-holes to aim from. Finish your snack and we'll go back to the hotel and hole up a spell."

As she did so he hailed their breed waitress and let her see he was a fair tipper before he mentioned their back way out. She said she didn't care which way they went if they were done. The other sisters working in the little steamy kitchen seemed to find their passage as amusing. Out back in the alley Fiona was blushing as she declared, "I'll bet they think the two of us are ducking my husband or your wife!"

He took her elbow with his left hand, leaving his gun hand free as he steered her between back fences and ash cans, soothing, "They may think I'm one of them horny rascals more interested in young boys. No offense but you don't look so married in them pants with your hair tucked up inside that high-crowned hat."

She laughed roguishly and allowed that made her feel safer about her virtue, adding, "I doubt any of those Cherokee ladies would recognize me in my Sunday bonnet and a proper dress in any case. Do you know where we are? I seem to be lost in this alley maze."

He pointed skyward with his chin and said, "The sun rises in the east and sets in the west, same as ever. I thought you said you knew how to survey, Miss Fiona."

She protested, "I do indeed and I hardly need a compass and transit to tell north from south in broad daylight. But that still doesn't tell me which way the Riverview Hotel may be from here!"

He reined her in near the far end of the alley and made sure the narrow side street they'd come to was clear, both ways, as he assured her, "That's nothing to bust out maps about. They call her the Riverview because she's a weed-grown lot away from the only river in these parts. Fort Smith's on a north-south bend of the Arkansas. So like the rest of the town we've got to be east of the hotel. The sun was shining in our faces as we left the hotel and it's beaming from behind and to the left of us right now, so figuring it has to be late afternoon . . ."

"I know where we are, now," she cut in as he steered her across the street and up yet another alley.

"So do I," he said. "I figure we ought to be able to work our way to the hotel stable without ever appearing on any important streets of Fort Smith."

She repressed a shudder and said, "You're scaring me again. But surely nobody after us could have expected us to duck out the back way back there, right?"

He said that was why they'd ducked out the back way and added, "I never said they were after you, Miss Fiona. It was *me* someone pegged a buffalo round at, just before we met."

She insisted, "After Captain Boyle vanished into thin air and all and all, you mean! Isn't it obvious someone's trying to prevent another government survey of that disputed border to the south?"

He shrugged and said, "Nobody I've talked to, yet, disputes the original survey all that much. They keep saying they'd like to make sure it ain't been shifted. Meanwhile we can't be certain Boyle vanished involuntary and sore losers

46

are always pegging shots at me. For in all modesty I've been riding for the Justice Department six or eight years and I've sent many a crook to prison or worse in that time."

She started to ask a another dumb question. Then she nodded and decided, "Keeping company with you could take years off a woman's life whether someone was out to prevent another survey or not. But if that attempt on your life near the courthouse had nothing to do with Captain Boyle's mission, how can you account for the simple fact that he's no longer here to survey?"

Longarm said, "I can't, yet. Whether we ever find out or not, the Choctaw Nation, the state of Arkansas, and the U.S. Government expect *some* damned body to run that survey. But we've already talked about slipping out of town discreet to carry out Captain Boyle's mission, with or without Captain Boyle."

She hesitated, stuck her chest out a mite, an inspiring sight, and said, "Well, I'm game to give it a try, even if I am a girl and all and all."

He said that was the spirit, idly wondering why she'd looked so boyish, before he'd gotten to thinking about being out on the trail with her, alone, for Lord-only-knew-how-long and how far they might be going.

Chapter 5

It seemed best to eat any apple one bite at a time and Fiona had already told him she'd given Captain Boyle a hard time for trying to make time with her at the hotel. So once they'd worked their way back inside, alive, he naturally identified himself as serious law to the desk clerk and tried to hire himself a room convenient to Fiona's.

They told him he couldn't have one anywhere in the fool hotel, thanks to all the old soldiers in town with their wives or someone else's. Fiona murmured something about them at least being safer up in her room while they figured out their next moves. Longarm didn't like the knowing look in the desk clerk's eyes. He knew assuring the priss he hardly ever trifled with young gals wearing men's pants before supper would only confirm the bastard's suspicions. So, attacking when many a many might be putting up his guard, Longarm said, "Captain Boyle, who seems to have vanished from your fourth floor, is under government protection as well. So who'd know best if he got called away by an urgent message, say late last night or early this morning?"

The clerk sniffed and said, "I wouldn't have been on duty at that hour. But we try to be up-to-date here at the Riverview."

He reached under the fake marble to produce a loose-leaf folder with a fake leather cover, opening it as he continued, "The night clerk's supposed to log any and all unusual events, the same as that fancy Parker House back East, for all its famous rolls and Turkish towels. So let's see and . . . Here it is, Deputy Long. A Western Union telegram, hand-delivered to this desk at a quarter to four this morning and naturally taken up to Captain Boyle by one of our own bellboys."

Longarm nodded knowingly and said he hoped the retired army engineer had proven a decent tipper at such an hour. Then he got out his own bitty notebook to note the time and the names of both hotel employees involved. As he and Fiona turned away to head for the stairwell she nudged him to whisper, "Custis, that snip we just talked to at the telegraph office was lying through her teeth!"

He softly replied, "I hate it when witnesses do that to me. I get more out of telegraph clerks who tell me Western Union don't allow 'em to give out information on paid-for messages. But how do you get the truth out of a pretty little thing who stares you smack in the eye with an innocent smile and, like you suggest, lies through her teeth?"

As he helped her up the stairs Fiona asked what might happen if they both went back to confront the snip with the simple testimony of both the night clerk and bellhop. He shrugged and replied, "She'd likely begin with the simple fact she wasn't on duty there at the time. There's an outside chance she was telling the truth as Western Union gave it to her to see. A lazy night clerk might have simply never logged one incoming message from Lord knows who, where, or what about. I've found on similar occasions that once a paper pusher messes up it's tough to get anyone to admit it. We could waste an awesome amount of time trying to change Western Union's story and, in the end, if they just hung tough, never know for certain."

They'd reached the second floor. Fiona pointed the way as she insisted they'd never find out where her boss had gone if nobody would even tell them where he might have gone, and why.

As they strode the corridor together he opined, "He'll doubtless wind up telling us about it, himself, if it was a legitimate wire from somebody decent. I'm more worried about a false message designed to lure him out into the predawn mists. Let's study on the sort of message it would take to sneak a man out of here at that hour, bag and baggage."

Fiona unlocked her door and ushered him into her corner room with built-in closets and bath, not bad for a Western county seat of modest size. She took off her big sombrero to shake down her luxurious mane of wavy blue-black hair with a relieved sigh, saying, "It would have had to be personal. Captain Boyle's shared all communications from the survey service with me since we've been out this way."

Longarm moved over to the windows, open and facing both north and west. Nothing sinister looked to be going on in the dusty streets below. The low afternoon sun was gilding the rippling surface of the broad, shallow Arkansas beyond the ragged tree tops of the overgrown and doubtless soggy lot they'd razed or just never built on over that way. He pulled the blinds, muttering, "It's best not to tempt fate when it could be packing a big fifty, good for better than a country mile. I see you got more than one lamp in here if the gloom bothers you, Miss Fiona."

She said there was plenty of light coming in around the edges and added, "I was about to say that afternoon sun was getting tiresome to my eyes and all and all. I know we're not supposed to, but I've been sweating like crazy in these manly riding clothes and I don't see how you men can stand it on a day like this one."

He said it wasn't easy as he removed his hat and asked her permit to hang up his frock coat as well. She suggested he get rid of his vest and shoestring tie while she, for one, would be after a quick dip in the tub and a change into something cooler if he didn't want to use the facilities first.

He told her to go ahead if she didn't mind him smoking. So she ducked in the bath and shut the door behind her as he fished out a cheroot, lit it, and since there didn't seem to be anything more proper, sat down on one end of her big brass bedstead.

He could tell she was running more than bath water in the privacy she had to work with. He was glad she was pragmatic about the simple facts of life. For even Queen Victoria had to get sweaty-crotched on a warm day and doubtless pissed, herself, on occasion. Like most late Victorians, Longarm had been raised not to comment or even notice the earthier details of a world still powered mostly by animal and human sweat. The modern plumbing of the Riverview Hotel allowed one to avoid an awesome amount of Victorian adjustments to natural body functions. But out on the trail in the squat-and-drop-it Ouachitas it would be way more comfortable in the company of a gal who could offer you first dibs on the crapper in such a natural, nonblushing manner. But that wasn't saying she'd invited him to act any more natural than that. She'd as much as warned him not to. Women usually meant it as a warning when they bragged about fending off other men. Of course, she'd told him Captain Boyle had been older than present company as well as way more married. So he thought about that as he smoked his cheroot most of the way down, idly wondering what all that splashing in there might mean. How much splashing did it take to wash even a sweaty crotch sweet again?

Then she came out, all rosy and wearing lots of lilac water and an ecru bathrobe of rough pongee silk Queen Victoria might not have approved of. The sort of flesh-colored robe covered all Fiona's important flesh, once you studied on it. The first effect was still just a tad inspiring. That mannish outfit had concealed her curves way more, and

51

turgid, nippled tits under flesh colored silk didn't look half as modest.

She sat down at the other end of the bedstead, saying the bath was all his, now. He said he'd wait 'til after supper, explaining, "Whether anyone with a buffalo rifle knows we're up here or not, it'll still be safer to send down to the hotel kitchen for some grub, let's say around sundown, seeing we had that coffee and cake this afternoon?"

She said sundown sounded about right. So he said he'd best keep his pants on 'til after, lest he get caught going down to order them some room service less formal.

She laughed easily but warned him not to get ideas about getting *too* comfortable. She said, "In the tub is one thing. But don't you have a change in your saddlebags, down below?"

He soberly replied, "I hardly ever traipse about in anything fancy as that pongee, Miss Fiona. I mean to change to denim trail duds before we leave and I've been thinking about the Winchester I left down in that tack room. Might fetch it when I go down to order our suppers. The hotel help can worry about getting the grub up those stairs. Is black hair and blue eyes natural to any particular part of Ireland, Miss Fiona?"

The Irish-American girl blinked her aquamarine eyes uncertainly and replied, "I've never been there. It's my mother's coloring I take after and she always said blue eyes and black hair were left over from the Shee or little people who dwelt in her old country before the fair Celts or red-haired raiders from the northern shores. Why do you ask? There are a lot of blue-eyed brunettes with Irish blood."

He got rid of his smoked-down cheroot as he observed, "I've noticed that. Boyle's as Irish a name as Coyne and, no offense, your kind's not inclined to marry up with Calvinists. Have you any idea what our missing surveyor's wife might look like?"

Fiona shook her head, saying she'd only met Himself a short time ago. She asked what Herself, doubtless still waiting for her man in Virginia City, could have had to do with his mysterious disappearance. When she said she'd never heard of a man's own wife having him abducted Longarm sighed and replied, "That's doubtless because you're not a lawman. You'd be surprised what some folk will do to their own parents, or kids, in this uncertain world. Were we talking about Virginia City, Nevada, or the smaller one in Montana, Miss Fiona?"

She thought and then said she was pretty sure the captain and his wife had been living in the one out Nevada way. When pressed she recalled he'd mentioned survey work along the east slopes of the Sierra Nevada, that his wife's name had been Maureen, which hardly sounded Mex, and that Boyle had never mentioned them having any kids. When she added Boyle had seemed to miss his apparently pretty Maureen an awful lot and that he'd in fact tried to excuse his drunken play for her with blarney about Irish eyes, Longarm decided, "Long shot and it raises more questions than it answers. But it's worth looking into if old Boyle remains among the missing overlong."

She asked him what he meant. He didn't want to talk dirty about other blue-eyed brunettes a man might miss a heap after younger and somewhat slimmer ones turned him down. He glanced at the golden light coming in around the blinds of the west window and muttered something about heading down to the hotel kitchen any time, now.

Fiona said, "It's too early for supper after all that cake and coffee. What's all this blather about Maureen Boyle of Virginia City, Nevada? Do you know her, Custis?"

He smiled back innocently—it wasn't easy—and replied, "Not from Virginia City, albeit anyone traveling east from there might well wind up on the Denver–Saint Lou run. After that, like I said, more questions than answers. Why would even a love-starved gent who'd sent for his love life sneak off to meet her when all he'd have to do was wait right here for her?"

Fiona shrugged inside her thin pongee and tried, "What if she was waiting for him somewhere else?"

53

Longarm gulped and decided, "Yep, a run up to K.C. in answer to most any excuse works pretty good. The timing of that telegram in the wee small hours is tight. But Western Union stays open all night and there was one within sight of the depot coffee shop, now that I study on it."

Fiona demanded, "Study on what, Custis? Did you meet Maureen Boyle somewhere before or not, and why would she wire the captain to meet her in Kansas City instead of here in Fort Smith?"

He had to look away as he mused, "Maybe she didn't want to meet him and, ah, the rest of us in Fort Smith." Then he frowned thoughtfully and added, "And maybe I'm playing chess when the name of the game is checkers. Once you get to considering everything that's *possible* you can miss the more simple and obvious. Somebody pegged a shot at me right here in Fort Smith and whoever did so couldn't have been Maureen Boyle no matter what she looks like or how she feels about long train rides. I'm going down to look at their supper menu, now. For early or not I'm feeling too proddy to just set and talk in circles."

He rose to his feet, leaving his hat, coat, and vest where they were but naturally leaving his sixgun on as she sort of purred at him to hurry back, since she was feeling sort of proddy, too.

Chapter 6

Proddy women tended to feel challenged by men with some control of their peckers. So Longarm took that leak at last in the hall pottery provided for guests in the cheaper rooms.

Downstairs, he planned his next few moves with forethought as well. He'd told Fiona not to open up to anyone 'til he got back. So he went out back to the stable to fetch his Winchester before he asked for any supper menu.

While he was there he decided he'd best unlash that bedroll from his McClellan. He'd found they made a man beg harder when they knew he had no place *else* to bed down. Then, shouldering his bulkier than heavy load, he went scouting for their supper.

The hotel diner opened off one end of the lobby, directly across from the archway leading into the tap room. They were singing up a storm in the tap room at this hour, even though the sunset was still in progress outside.

Things seemed more sedate in the dining room, albeit he was glad he and Fiona had decided on room service. Just about every table was taken and there were snippy reservation signs on the few left. A snippy waiter who likely squatted to pee came over, staring suspiciously at Longarm's bare head, shirtsleeves, and shoulder load. He said they only served gents in proper attire.

Longarm smiled thinly and explained he didn't want them to serve him a gent in any sort of attire, adding, "I want a proper supper for two sent up to Room 207. So you'd best let me look at your menu, first."

The waiter, who must have been the straw boss, snapped his fingers at a younger one and said to fetch a menu. But, before he could, all hell seemed to be busting loose behind Longarm. So he dropped his bedroll smack in the dining room entrance and whirled about to advance on the sound of the guns on the far side of the lobby, levering a round into the chamber of his Winchester before he got to the entrance to the tap room, calling out in a tone of command, "Cease and desist in the name of the law! That's me, the law."

But as he swept the smoke-filled tap room with his eyes and gun muzzle he could see it was already just about over. A middle-aged man in the faded full dress of a Union officer lay spread all over the sawdust near the upright piano, staring up at the pressed tin ceiling with his mouth agape and blood still running out of one ear, albeit not under pressure this late in the game. The .36 Colt conversion on the floor near his limp right hand was still smoking.

A younger fool in the butternut uniform of a Confederate enlisted man reclined more like a painting of Cleopatra against the brass rail along the base of the bar. He was still gripping his old Le Mat revolver. The French had sold a lot of arms to the South and the Le Mat was still an awesome weapon in the hands of a man with strong enough wrists. The retired reb who'd only hit his man once for all that blasting was just as dead, whether he wanted to smile like that about the bloody front of his tunic or not. Nobody else had a weapon drawn. An amiable breed dressed more vaquero than veteran volunteered, "It was over musical tastes, Sheriff. The old boy in blue wanted to hear 'Marching Through Georgia' played in A-Flat. Old Ike, there, who rode for the Slash Eleven when he wasn't dressed nostalgic over the Battle of Pea Ridge, took a mighty firm stand against the notion, with the results you see."

Longarm was saved further fooling with a local matter by the timely arrival of two Fort Smith lawmen, followed in due course by old Prince Maledon, who'd been headed home for his own supper when he'd heard someone disturbing hell out of the peace.

Longarm told the old hangman there was nobody there for the federal government to hang, or even arrest, and added he'd been in the process of ordering grub when the poor assholes had decided never to eat again. Maledon followed him outside, saying, "Just as well I run across you, anyways. One of our deputies, canvassing the neighborhood, got a possible albeit half-ass description of that cuss who tried to put you on a forever-diet, earlier."

Longarm brightened and asked to hear more. So Prince said, "Face shaded by his broad-ass hat brim. Hat gray with its crown crushed North Plains style, like your own."

"I've made lots of friends out Colorado way," Longarm sighed.

Maledon shrugged and said, "He could be wearing his hat another way, now. The one on *our* side, a dressmaker peering out her window suspicious at a stranger loitering below it, betwixt her building and the next, says he was head to toe in a gray poplin travel duster, which she naturally described in more detail than the rifle he was packing, cradled,'til you come along. But she ain't disputing it could have been a Sharps Big Fifty. She heard it go off. She stuck herself with a needle when it did. But he'd run off by the time she got back to her window. So she's not willing to swear under oath the stranger loitering below her window pegged shot-one at you, direct."

Longarm grimaced and replied, "I doubt we could make an arrest on such a describing in any case. I wish Frank and Jesse hadn't invented riding into town in all sorts of weather under rain slickers or travel dusters."

Maledon nodded and opined, "There ought to be a law against both. All a crook has to do, once he's done something dirty, is shuck that head to toe disguise and offer to ride with the posse, dressed like somebody else entire. They figure that's how Frank and Jesse got away, that time up Northfield way."

Longarm was too polite to reply he'd just said that. By now they'd made it back to the entrance to the dining room. His bedroll seemed to be missing. But in the end, after he and the old hangman had parted friendly again, the hired help produced his rolled bedding and even a bentwood chair to sit in whilst he perused their menu.

He ordered steak and potatoes with apple pie along with rat cheese and plenty of coffee, figuring Fiona would likely go along with that if she et halfway normal.

They told him they'd tote it up to them in say twenty minutes. So he toted his bedroll and Winchester on up to wait for them.

He and Fiona had agreed ahead on a sneaky knock. But he'd barely started before she'd flung the door open, sort of wild-eyed and tear-streaked, to haul him inside and climb all over him, sobbing about hearing gunshots and just about giving up on him ever getting back to her alive.

He kicked the door shut behind him and let his bedroll and rifle go anywhere they wanted as he somehow wound up across the bed with the worried little thing, kissing away her tears as he explained how he'd come through that replay of the War Between the States without a scratch. She seemed to enjoy having her tears kissed away and he was sincerely sorry he'd ordered room service for them by the time he heard someone rapping on their chamber door and rolled off the bed, and Fiona, to answer it.

The door naturally shut on a spring lock. That gave him a polite excuse to call out, "Just a minute whilst I figure this fool lock. Who's out there, our supper?"

The voice replying "Western Union telegram for Miss Coyne" sounded innocent enough. Longarm still had his .44-40 out, if politely down his right pants leg, as he opened up.

There was really a uniformed bellhop there, too cool a hand to let on he was surprised to see how Miss Fiona Coyne had grown a mustache as he held out the yellow envelope on a German silver salver.

Knowing wires were usually paid for at the other end Longarm tipped the kid a generous dime and shut the door in his face. He handed the envelope to the brunette on the bed as he sat back down beside her.

Fiona opened it, scanned the message, and handed it to him to read, even as she said, as if he couldn't read, "Captain Boyle's superiors have caught more complaints and want to know how we're coming with that survey. You said something about getting them to entrust me with the chore, Custis?"

He nodded, reading just enough to see she'd phrased things about right as he replied, "I said it would be only decent to give the man twenty-four hours to explain his odd behavior. He'll likely be fired if it turns out he run off to tend private beeswax on time he's being paid for by the survey service. If we have to turn him in, I don't foresee a big fuss over you carrying on in his place."

She pouted, "I'm a girl. You know how some men feel about my kind doing their kind of work."

Longarm nodded but soothed, "Somebody has to resurvey that old line poco tiempo and you're on the scene as Boyle's chosen assistant with all them trade school degrees."

He didn't want to be caught kissing her some more by room service so he added, "That reminds me. I meant to ask you why a graduate surveyor would want a degree in Botany."

She asked, "Isn't it obvious? That's why Captain Boyle asked for me when he saw it on my application papers. I took the extra credits because some knowledge of botany can be helpful in the field and all and all. The flora and even the fauna can tell you things about the earth beneath your feet that can save you mucking about with streak plates and acid. For example, hydrangea blossoms blue over iron-rich soil and pink where there's none at all. Kentucky blue grass, a grass of the old world if the truth be known, only grows where the soil has plenty of lime, while plumbago, of course . . ."

"I've heard prospectors tell of indicator weeds," he cut in. Then he added with a satisfied nod, "Boyle's picking you makes a heap of sense as soon as one recalls them witness trees someone's trifled with. Anyone with a botany degree would be tough to fool with a tree too young to have been blazed and recorded back before the Mexican War."

"Or the wrong species," she volunteered. "As we've all agreed, using anything as impermanent as a growing tree for a halfway permanent bench mark is asking for just the sort of trouble the captain and me were sent out here to deal with. Most so-called witness trees are recorded by less professional claim stakers. I understand there's a dearth of decent outcroppings in those parts of the Ouachitas in question. But nevertheless the trees chosen by the original team should have been prominent oaks rather than shorter lived pines or, God forbid, alders, poplars, or even gums!"

Longarm nodded sagely and said, "I can follow your drift and I ain't even got a botany degree. Alder lasts as fence-posting, once it's been cut and cured, but it sure grows loco for reading material whilst it's alive, and poplar ain't even good for burning. What's wrong with gum? Seems to me we had us some mighty old gum trees all about in West-by-God-Virginia and some had grown prominent enough to stand out."

She shook her head and insisted, "Oaks. There are well over forty-odd varieties of oak in the Arkansas hills, all superior to almost any timber this side of tropical hardwoods for permanence."

Longarm agreed he'd hardly risk bench-marking anything but an oak if there were that many kinds of oaks to choose from. Then the room service help was at the door with their supper on a rolling supper table with white linen and all. So Longarm shifted his rifle and bedroll out of their way and tipped a whole quarter when they set the table up next to the bed. The bellhop in charge must have noticed Fiona was already down to that bathrobe. He neither grinned nor met Longarm's eye when he said they could send for someone to haul away the table and dirty dishes any time they wanted.

Fiona agreed with Longarm's selections from the hotel menu as they ate side by side, seated on her bed. Having been exposed to higher education, or mayhaps simply because of her gender, the gal liked to go on talking whilst they et.

Longarm had been raised to be polite as well as a mite more direct about his meals in, say, an army mess tent or cow town beanery. So he was able to jaw and chaw without choking if that was what a gal he was supping with wanted. This one kept fretting about being a woman as well as a well-trained surveyor, cuss their stuffy hides.

So, washing down some tender beef and sort of tough potatoes with black coffee, he soothed, "They *hired* you, didn't they? That wire just told you they were getting anxious and, no offense, I suspect I could handle the chore myself if push came to shove. I took the liberty of regarding the map as I was leaving Denver. From your bench mark here in Forth Smith the original survey team run the line due south to the Red River along the same longitude, right?"

She shook her unbound head becomingly as she replied, "Wrong. I agreed they *should* have. But they somehow erred along the way and hit the Red River a good five statute miles to the west. Nobody noticed, or perhaps nobody cared, until the lawful boundaries of the Indian Nation were fixed forever in granite, or perhaps map paper would be most accurate and all and all."

He whistled dubiously. She insisted, "I have an extra survey map to let you play with all you like, if you think I don't know what I'm talking about. Without looking at any map I'd be willing to bet you the line starts just south of here—*east* of 94°-30′ west while they bench-marked it that far *west* of 94°-30′ west on the north shore of the Red River. They may have been running a compass course through rough country instead of the right way, with a transit. Or maybe they just didn't know how to use a transit. Andrew Jackson would have appointed them and he *was* the darling politician who first announced that the spoils should go to the victor."

Longarm dug into his dessert, recalling but not saying Old Hickory's old woman had dipped snuff, to hear their admirers tell. The pie was good and the tangy rat cheese cut the sweetness just right. He swallowed some coffee as well and asked what made those witness trees so all-fired important if the survey service had its fool line mapped good enough to show a five-mile drift in a beeline of at least a hundred and thirty-odd miles.

She said, "You can tuck nearly a whole township into such a modest deviation. But we don't leave bench marks the length of a survey line to catch mistakes of old surveyors. The Bureau of Land Management, Bureau of Indian Affairs, War Department, and all and all depends on our bench marks to avoid *future* errors. A homesteader filing a claim or an army engineer laying out an outpost can hardly be expected to do so with his own transit and chronometer after we've been paid to make it easier. We try to leave a mapped and numbered bench mark at least every fifteen minutes in country open to settlement and . . ."

"Minutes?" Longarm frowned uncertainly, shoving back from his demolished dessert to regard her from one elbow as she explained, "Minutes or fractions of a degree of latitude or longitude. One degree is a little under sixty miles or a bit much to work with without precision instruments, so . . ."

"It's coming back to me, now," he cut in. "I know about them fancy Frenchified notions we should have all our weights and measures round out to fractions of the waistline of Mother Earth. But I was riz on rods, furlongs, old-fashioned country miles, and such."

She nodded and shoved the wheeled table away to half-recline beside him, saying, "Spoken like a member of the public we're paid to serve. Given a bench-marked outcrop or witness tree to start with, less-skilled surveys can be run well enough for your average county court with simple country methods. But a property line could be off by yards, if not miles, starting with no bench mark or, worse yet, a *false* one left by someone who . . . Why do you suppose anyone would *want* to, Custis?"

He shrugged his free shoulder and said that was what he was being paid to find out whilst she found the righteous beeline to the Red River. It was getting darker by the minute and unless someone lit a street lamp just outside her windows he was going to have to get up and light that globe lamp closer to the head of the bed. If they wanted any light, leastways. He decided it would be more polite to let her decide. He said, "Seeing you know the hills we're headed into at least as good as me, have you ever heard tell of gold in them there hills?"

She laughed she was getting harder to see, now, as she replied, "Not on this side of the line. The Indian Nation hasn't been prospected as thoroughly. Arkansas may have one diamond outcrop, down in Pike County. They're still arguing about whether they're real or whether there are enough to justify a mine. There doesn't seem to be any gold or silver anywhere in the state. There's some coal and there may be some rock oil worth drilling for, but the original survey recorded no mineral finds of any interest along the line we'll be running and what's that you're running along my thigh, sir?"

He stopped what he'd been doing but left his hand in place as he said, "Just trying to make sure you're still there. Would you feel better about it if I lit the bed lamp?"

She patted the back of that same hand, soothingly, to reply she hadn't been planning on reading in bed. So he chuckled and said, "I don't think Drake had struck the first rock oil in Penn State when they were blazing witness trees of Andy Jackson. But there's no way we can delve for unsuspected mineral wealth before we *get* down yonder."

She let herself fall all the way to the bed covers on her back as she sort of purred, "What *are* you delving for, then, and why are you teasing us both so on your way there?"

He lay flatter, sliding his free hand higher 'til, noticing her thighs were crossed with some of that thin but stout pongee blocking further progress, he answered, honestly, "I haven't been out to tease us, Miss Fiona. But you said you'd already had it out with Captain Boyle on this very subject and I seldom hunt beyond no trespassing signs, so . . ."

"*A mo mala* he was older and uglier with a wife besides!" She cut in, opening her thighs and robe in welcome as she guided his big hand to her little moist clit as he rolled closer to kiss her some more as he commenced to slide two fingers back and forth, then in and out, in company with her soft moans of pleasure.

It would have been way tougher to go further without awkward pauses had she not began to use her own skilled hands with obviously practiced skill. Once she'd unbuckled or unbuttoned everything that needed it and hauled out his stiff organ grinder to offer it proper guidance, he was atop her and in her just right within seconds and not a second too soon, judging from how quickly she seemed to be coming, moving her slender athletic hips in time with his every thrust in that mind-reading way of the enthusiastic natural screwer, male or she-male.

It got even better, once they'd enjoyed some howdy coming and took time out to strip down entire and shove two pillows under her spunky, bare behind. There was just enough light to make out her pale flesh and jet hair, at both ends. So he was able to contrast this blue-eyed Irish gal with

64

Magnolia, or Maureen, the night before, and whoever might have said you got more variety by switching from blondes to brunettes or even gringo to Mex had simply never mounted such different Irish types in succession. They even smelled and tasted different. But once he'd come in this one thrice and they were sort of showing off, he was able to pound Fiona harder by shutting his eyes and raising most of his weight off her, pretending she was the softer and riper Magnolia 'til, falling back down against her firmer, younger body, he felt reinspired about both of them.

For he'd long since decided nine out of ten women were swell in bed whilst the tenth was worth bedding for the novelty, Lord love 'em all, and it seemed a shame he only got to do this with one blue-eyed brunette at a time. So as he rutted with Fiona he idly wondered who Magnolia, or Maureen, might be rutting with this very moment.

With all respect due this one, and she surely deserved it, the missing Captain Boyle was doubtless enjoying himself as much, right now, if he'd really run off to be with his Maureen-Magnolia, and what else worked any better? Boyle hadn't been able to get at this one and he must have recalled the other as fondly, if that had been his wife, and who else would have acted as odd after learning some romance on a cross-country train was heading the same way to meet up with the same husband?

Thinking distracted a man who'd already come that many times in a row and Fiona seemed to require a breather as well. So he suggested they share a smoke and rolled off to light up when she said she needed a pee even more.

He was glad they were on such natural terms, now. Traveling alone with a gal and four shitting and pissing ponies on open range where a body just had to dismount and do it, sooner or later, could be a real pain unless both parties knew each other well enough to admit human feelings. As he listened to her tinkle in the dark whilst he lay smoking, the pillow stinking friendly from her love sweat, he felt tempted to get even more personal when she came back. But when

65

she did he held off asking her whether she'd considered all the disadvantages of days and nights on the trail with a boss she wasn't screwing, and he didn't think he ought to mention that other Irish gal at all. For some gals could get jealous as all get-out after they'd been screwed a mite and he knew she'd be unable to tell him whether he'd screwed Captain Boyle's woman or not, even if he made her mad at him. Magnolia Gray might have simply been a crazy lady as well as a great lay.

Fiona came back to lay him great some more, her sweet little love maw cool and wet from some sink splashing, bless her.

He toyed with it while he finished his cheroot, not to be cheap but to recover his strength and do it right. She laid her head sweetly on his bare shoulder and toyed back, more friendly than passionate, as she purred, "I'm glad we'll be starting out as established lovers, darling. I was worried about our times ahead on the trail, and to tell the truth that's the only justification I can see for the idea of all-male armies, cattle drives, and all and all."

He patted her bare shoulder with the hand he didn't have in her lap, observing, "I tried to have that out with a devotee of Miss Virginia Woodhull, the suffragette leader. She seemed to feel it was unfair to deny womankind the enjoyments of combat service on the field of battle. I don't know why. I saw battlefield service in the war and *I* never felt deprived when they told me I could quit. My point wasn't about fighting or dying as much as it was distractions, though. I tried to tell her folk on the field of battle, male or she-male, have to forget all about personal privacy as they share the same quarters, shell holes and all, for days at a time."

He took a thoughtful drag on his smoke before musing, "I don't know. Mayhaps if everyone in the squad got to mount the same she-male squad leader, any time they felt like it, the distractions of such intimacy wouldn't cause anyone's mind to wander out on picket duty where a soldier has enough to keep his mind to."

Fiona kissed the hollow of his collarbone and demurely asked whether he or she would be the squad leader, should Captain Boyle fail to return.

He got rid of his smoked-down cheroot to kiss her back better before saying, "You survey folk are in charge of the surveying. My job's just to keep anyone from interfering and, maybe, find out who interfered with the ones who've gone before you."

By now they were stroking one another hard enough to feel little further need for conversation. But just as he was shoving those pillows back under her firm hips someone knocked on her door, firmly.

They both froze, of course. Then someone softly called out, "You in there, Deputy Long?" So Longarm was off the bed and over by the door, naked as a jay but gun in hand as he cautiously called back, "Mebbe. Who's out there and what might you want with him?"

Their early-evening caller replied, "I'm Deputy Hardwick. Prince Maledon thought you ought to know. Wasn't you looking for that army engineer, Captain Boyle?"

Longarm felt a big gray cat get up and turn around a time or two in his stomach as he quietly replied, "I surely have been. What about him?"

It didn't help much when the other lawman called back, "They just found him stone cold dead, five or six miles north in Crawford County. Somebody shot him in the head with a big fifty. They identified the body by the contents of its pockets. A big fifty don't leave you much of a face to go by, you know."

Chapter 7

Once Longarm got dressed and over to the Fort Smith morgue with the slim, laconic Deputy Hardwick, he decided, first off, that his fellow lawman wasn't given to hyperbole. The somewhat overweight and very pallid body lying nude atop a zinc table under a fizzing pressure lamp was mighty messed-up. There'd have been way more to its face if the buffalo round had entered from the front. But Boyle, if this was Boyle, had been shot from behind, at close range, the muzzle blast singeing away a circle of graying brown hair above the nape of the plump neck, and then the big, soft slug had torn most of the face away on departing at about where the bridge of the cadaver's nose might have been, taking along a heap of bone and brain matter as well.

Longarm had told Fiona to let him handle this, hoping to spare her rep as well as her feelings. But he was just as glad she showed up, in a summer print dress and straw boater, by the time they'd determined no baggage had been found near the body. Two colored boys had found the body that afternoon, wrapped half around one pier of a railroad trestle just north of town. Longarm had agreed the baggage of a man who'd departed Fort Smith by rail in the wee, small hours could have gone on by rail to Lord-only-knew-where. But Longarm was against an all-points on Captain Boyle's baggage before they knew this poor soul had been Captain Boyle.

Then Fiona Coyne came in to gasp, cover her face with her hands, and turn away, sobbing, "It's Himself. But Mary, Mother of God, what have they done to the poor man?"

Longarm met the eyes of Hardwick, on the far side of the garishly illuminated cadaver, as he said, "He was shot by a person or persons unknown, Miss Fiona. We're still working on whether there was a train out at the right time, or how come nobody aboard saw fit to report the detonation of a mighty big buffalo gun on board if there was."

He turned to an older man who'd already been introduced to him as the county coroner, asking, "Could you make an educated guess as to how long he lay there before those more helpsome boys found him, Doc?"

The part-time coroner and full-time undertaker grimaced and said, "No. I wasn't there when those well-meaning but pestiferous colored boys hauled him up the clay bank and let him lay Lord-knows-how-long in the sun whilst they went to fetch a buckboard. You judge how long a fairly fresh body may have been dead by its, ah, rectal temperature. Sorry, ma'am. Those boys can't recall whether this body was fully submerged, partly submerged, or high and dry after lying Lord-knows-how-long in how much sunshine or shadow under that trestle. We know he was alive and well less than a full twenty-four hours ago. So pick a time that goes with a suspect and I'll back your play in court, boys."

Longarm smiled thinly and declared, "That's easier said than done. A blurry cuss in a pork-pied hat and ankle-length gray duster may or may not have pegged a shot at me with a big fifty. Well after gunning this poor cuss, if we're discussing the same rascal with the same gun."

Hardwick opined they had to be. It turned out he was the one who'd found that old seamstress for Prince Maledon. He said the old hangman was at home right now but full-dressed if anything more interesting developed this evening.

Longarm said, "Well, if you're asking me for suggestions I'd commence with Western Union, who seems to have fibbed to us this afternoon unless two whole hotel employees are lying through their teeth for less reason."

He brought everyone there up-to-date on the little more he and Fiona knew. She backed him, albeit nobody had any call to doubt a thing he said.

He left out the dirty parts about himself and Boyle's Maureen, if Magnolia had been Maureen. The coroner said they'd naturally want to get in touch with the dead man's kith and kin. So Longarm put mysterious brunettes aboard night trains on the back of the stove for now. If the dead man's wife turned out to have never left home, he'd been playing slap and tickle with someone *else's* wife, most likely. Either way, he couldn't see a wife wiring a loving husband to meet her somewhere else to spare his feelings, and then murdering him with a big fifty. So what worked better?

The local lawmen, federal and county, seemed to be working together smart enough. So Longarm put other possible fibbers on the back of the stove as well, announcing he'd been sent there to ride herd on witness trees. They agreed they'd as likely catch the killer of Captain Boyle if he hung around Fort Smith with that big fifty. They seemed to feel Longarm and Fiona's plan to carry on without Boyle a swell way to get killed as well as the best way to smoke out anyone anxious to prevent another survey. Hardwick protested, "At least ask Prince for some armed and dangerous help, Longarm. We know you're good and mayhaps this little lady is tougher than she looks, but Jumping Judas . . ."

"I doubt Prince has the authority to detail armed escorts in his superior's absence." Longarm cut in. And nodding at the dead man's duds piled atop another table, he continued, "We can't be certain Boyle was gunned over witness trees.

70

He should have had at least a little money on him unless robbery was the motive. So did he?"

The coroner nodded and said, "Close to a hundred in paper and thirty in specie. Had a nice Ingersol watch, and a wedding band worth at least ten dollars as well. We were well ahead of you, there. Unless they were after something in his baggage, leastways."

Longarm grimaced and said, "We don't know for certain his baggage traveled that far north with him. You boys said you meant to jaw with the railroad about such matters. So, meanwhile, Miss Fiona and me had best get cracking in the other direction."

Nobody tried to stop them. As they strode the dark streets back to the hotel, he told Fiona he wanted her to get set for some serious riding as he paid one last call on Western Union. When she demurely suggested he keep her company while she stripped down to change, he laughed and said, "It'll be just as romantic out on the trail, once we clear Fort Smith and the surrounding truck farms entire by starlight."

When she asked how hard and long a night ride they were talking about, he explained, "As far and as fast as we can manage by sunrise. I'll tell you as we ride through it just how cluttered up the range to the south has got since last I rode it. I know cheek-by-jowl chicken spreads, hog farms, and bean fields extend at least five miles around any produce market worth mention. Dairy operations will be just beyond the garbage-fed hogs and chickens, and how much range beef we'll encounter after that depends on how ambitious new nesters have been with their Green River axes and Toledo crosscuts. The Homestead Act can only do so much in country cluttered with wild timber or dense Indians."

They parted at the hotel. He warned her not to go down to the stable alone before he returned. Then he turned away to leg it over to Western Union.

He circled some to make sure he wasn't being followed. It was still just after midnight when he sashayed in to find the middle-aged night man alone behind the counter with a dog-eared and back-dated copy of *Strand Magazine.* Longarm admired *Strand,* even if they did spell some words odd in London Town. Their adventure stories made sense and on the occasions they'd mentioned the American West they'd got things less wild than, say, Ned Buntline.

As the telegraph clerk put his magazine aside to see what his late-night caller had in mind they both recognized each other. Longarm nodded and said, "I'm sure glad we had that collision out in Nevada that time, pard. It saves us both a heap of bullshit about company wires strung across federal lands and to hell with company policy, right?"

The old-timer he'd had it out with in the past sighed wearily and replied, "What can I do for you, Longarm? Frank and Jesse ain't been by this evening to wire home, but . . ."

"Captain Boyle of Virginia City, where last we met, and the U.S. Survey Service, sending or receiving. Your turn."

The Western Union man made a wry face and replied, "Nothing this evening. We only keep carbons 'til they commence to pile up. But I can tell you he wired home and, let's see, their branch office in Saint Lou two or three days ago. Wait, he cashed a money order day before yesterday and we keep records *that* important indefinite."

He had to go in the back to rummage in the files. When he came back he placed the carbon copy of a Western Union money order on the countertop between them, saying, "Here you go. Two hundred and fifty dollars from his home office. Message attached tells him to watch it because he's been expending faster than his expense allotments were calculated. Man could get awesomely drunk in this town on two hundred and fifty dollars. Wouldn't have to drink alone, neither, unless he wanted to."

Longarm thought before he decided, "He had most half of it on him and even if he hadn't we're talking more drinking money than killing money."

That inspired the telegraph clerk to ask who'd been killed. Longarm muttered, "So much for urgent inquiries to railroad dispatchers," and tersely brought Western Union up-to-date as he peeled some telegram blanks from the handy counter pad and proceeded to block in messages that should have gone out already.

The clerk agreed the mysterious gunning of Captain Boyle was right mysterious but defended his fellow Fort Smithers by pointing out, "Judge Parker can get awesomely cranky when his boys even fart without his permit. Western Union will still be proud to send anything you want sent to anybody, though, since you're taking the tanning if you're exceeding your authority."

Longarm started another wire to yet another government office as he growled, "I don't work for Isaac Parker. We both work for the U.S. Department of Justice, whether he thinks he runs it or not. I ain't doing everything for him and his boys. I just want some things looked into for me, personal, as I ride south a ways. While you're being so helpsome, have you sent any messages for a Miss Fiona Coyne, pretty young brunette with blue eyes?"

The clerk nodded and said, "Sure. When she first got here, around the first of the week. You're right about her being pretty. She wired her folk in Saint Lou that she was out our way, safe and sound. That's about it. She never wired home for money. Can't recall us delivering anything less important to her."

Longarm nodded and said, "She's struck me as truthsome, so far. But whilst we're on the subject of late-night deliveries, they tell me at the hotel a wire was delivered to Captain Boyle around four in the morning, going on twenty-odd hours ago. Your day clerk told me they were full of it. So who's full of it, her or them?"

The clerk said, flatly, "Them. I was on duty last graveyard shift, just as I'm on duty this one. We never received any telegram for your Captain Boyle. So how could we have delivered one to his durned hotel?"

Longarm said he couldn't see how, either, but insisted, "I'd still like to talk about how such wires get delivered, when, and if they do come in that late."

The clerk shrugged, turned away, and called out, "Skeeter! Front and center!"

Then, sure enough, a sleepy-looking colored boy of about fourteen came out from the back, smothering a yawn. The clerk ordered him to tell this other gent how he went about delivering late-night telegrams. Skeeter looked confused and blurted, "I just carry 'em where you tells me to take 'em, suh. You ast me when you hired me did I know my fool way around Fort Smith and I ain't got lost yet, has I?"

The clerk told Longarm, "Skeeter's all right, for all his uppity sass. Born free. Knows how to read house numbers and moves faster than one might think, just looking at him."

Longarm questioned the boy in a friendlier tone. Skeeter assured him and Longarm believed he'd never delivered any mysterious messages to the late Captain Boyle. The clerk dismissed the young messenger and said he'd get Longarm's wires off at night letter rates when he damn well felt like it. That was why night letter rates were so much cheaper. They were sent at the convenience of Western Union to be delivered the next day instead of fast as possible. Longarm figured anyone asleep at this hour would find tomorrow morning a less alarming time to receive a telegram than say half an hour from now. Poor Captain Boyle had doubtless been as confused as edified by whatever that had been in the wee small hours.

If anyone was tailing him on the nearly deserted streets after midnight they were damned good. Back at the hotel Longarm found a key clerk he'd never spoken to before on duty. Longarm flashed his ID and when the late-night room wrangler allowed he knew about Miss Coyne having a guest in her single, but what the hell, Longarm snapped a silver dollar on the fake marble between them, soothing, "We weren't trying to screw you out of my night's lodgings and as a matter of fact neither one of us will be staying the whole hire of Room 207. But now that we're such pals, let's talk about your last shift and a telegram some say you sent up to Captain Boyle while others say you never."

The clerk made the silver dollar vanish. They both knew the management would never see a cent of it. Then he shrugged and said, "Some county deputies already asked us about that. You can talk to Willy, the same bellhop, when he comes back down. I was jawing with some other guests right about here when the Western Union messenger whipped in and out down at that end of the counter. He left the sealed message on the counter. Next time Willy passed through I told him to take it on up to whoever it was addressed to. He said, later, Captain Boyle stiffed him on the tip he was expecting. That's how I know it was Captain Boyle. As I told those other lawmen, I never even looked at the infernal wire."

Longarm nodded and said, "Let's not worry about how authentic the yellow envelope looked. How would you describe the messenger who left it?"

The clerk pursed his lips and decided, "Uninteresting. Like I said, I was talking to some good old boys about a traveling salesman and this old farmer with a pretty young wife and an ugly daughter."

Longarm said, "I've heard that one. I don't suppose you'd recall whether the messenger was colored or not?"

The clerk blinked thoughtfully and said, "He wasn't. Leastways, I don't *think* he was. He had on a broad-brimmed hat and you can see how dim the lobby is at this hour."

Longarm said, "The messenger working the graveyard shift for the telegraph office right now seems to get about without no hat. He's got on a checked cotton shirt and white duck pants."

The clerk shook his head and said, "Neither. The one last night might have been wearing most any sort of shirt and pants for all I could make out. He had on one of them summer-weight dusters, light tan or gray, I reckon.

75

I'm pretty sure he was a white but don't hold me to that if he turns out to have been a breed or, hell, a grass-green frog prince if it's all that *important* to you."

Longarm sighed and said, "It's important as hell, but as you just suggested, it's best to keep an open mind 'til I get a better look at the son of a bitch!"

Chapter 8

By the time the sky was pearling rosy to their east Longarm and Fiona were more than a dozen miles south of Fort Smith with their half dozen ponies. Captain Boyle had hired four to carry and pack for him and his assistant. Longarm had insisted they bring what Fiona called the leftover saddle bronc along, toting its fair share of the surveying and camping shit Boyle had amassed while waiting for their armed escort.

Longarm disagreed with his fellow deputies as to how many gun hands the new survey might need in unsettled country to the south. But he found it odd the dead man had planned on running a new beeline with that slight but important deviation to the west with only one assistant, however able.

Fiona hadn't argued when he'd pointed out that Mason and Dixon had brought along a whole raft of less famous help to hold survey poles, pitch tents, peel spuds, and so on. She said she'd mentioned that a time or two but that Boyle had told her to let him worry about it while she reminded him so much of his pretty Maureen.

There were three main routes running more or less due south in line with the less visible eastern border of the Indian Nation. There were north-south wagon traces, used by red or whites inside or outside the unfenced confines of the Nation, or Arkansas if you wanted to be picky the other way. The third clear route to the south, starting inside the western limits of Arkansas, was of course the railroad right-of-way. That was the one Longarm had chosen for their night ride out of Fort Smith. It would have been less practical had they been hauling so much shit by buckboard. But ponies saw better than folk in the dark and only needed those few inches betwixt the ends of the railroad ties and the drop-off to make fair time single file on long lead lines. They were moving through some second growth hardwood, mostly cottonwood and other weed trees, when Longarm heard the distant moaning of a locomotive at a crossing and called back to Fiona, "I was hoping for another mile or more by sunrise but we'd best quit while we're ahead. Follow me tight and watch out for the telegraph pole down the berm just ahead."

She called back she saw it. Then they were busy a spell, getting themselves and the less willing stock off the tracks to a modest clearing Longarm had read by considering tree tops against the lighter sky rather than the still dark woods more directly ahead.

As Fiona rode up beside him in the wider space that train he'd meant to avoid rumbled past, unseen by them at this distance and vice versa. When he said so Fiona asked, "A mo mala. Do you really think the killer of poor Captain Boyle would be following after us with murderous intent aboard a railroad train?"

To which he replied, with a thin smile, "Remind me never to rob a bank with you, kitten. There were telegraph poles as well as railroad tracks back yonder. You'd be surprised what one can scout from a moving train and wire back along the line. The Pinkertons have nailed many an owlhoot rider that way and some Indians are pretty dumb about trains as well. We'll do well to average forty miles a night in these saddles. Trains roll farther than that in just an hour while, as for the speed of dots or dashes along an electrified wire . . ."

She said she could see *what* he'd been worried about if he'd kindly inform her *who* they might be worried about. He said, "I'm still working on that. Anyone can see they go together to some extent. Whether the sneaks cutting down witness trees are the same ones who gunned your boss or not remains to be seen. Meanwhile I figure we're close to where the rails cross over into the Indian Nation and that's where I'd set up an ambush if *I* was murderous. So we'd best stay out of sight in this tanglewood 'til it's dark again and slip across a tad south of the tracks."

Fiona couldn't argue as he dismounted and commenced to tether all the stock he'd been leading to saplings. But by the time she'd done as much and he'd unsaddled his ponies to move over and start helping her with the others, she'd had time to ponder and so she asked him how come they had to cross over into the Indian Nation if the survey line they were checking out ran simply along one edge.

He explained, "Ain't following that line, yet. Want to get down to where it's seriously disputed without getting either of us backshot. Correct me if I'm wrong, but doesn't all that bull about witness trees commence in the wooded Ouachita Mountains, a good fifty miles or more from here?"

She laughed wearily and declared he'd know better than she where they were, adding, "Captain Boyle said we had to double-check about a dozen miles where the line lies straight on the map but climbs up and over the Rich Mountain Ridge."

Longarm nodded and said, "There you go. I've been studying the map as well. The country of which you speak is too busted up for railroads or even dirt roads. Lord only knows who could be out to steal any of it from either the red or white ridge runners down near Rich Mountain. Meanwhile the railroad tracks offer easier passage almost that far on the

Indian side of the line before whipping back on this side just a whoop and a holler from Rich Mountain, itself. They got a flag stop down that way named after said mountain. We'll turn off the tracks way sooner, where there's no town at all, to commence your new survey up and over. I'll let you figure that part out. If I'd been Captain Boyle I'd have hired at least a couple more hands."

As he broke out some nose bags for their tethered ponies she told him she would have as well. Then she decided, "Maybe he meant to simply search for the original bench marks and sight from one to the next. You're right about a survey from scratch calling for one out front with an aiming pole while the other adjusts the cross hairs and all and all."

He began to fill a nose bag from a water bag as he mused partly to himself, "None of us would be here at all if the complaints hadn't been about bench marks shifted mighty sneaky. Try her this way. Boyle's own boss was concerned he'd been running up a heap of field expenses. Now look about and tell me how much of the taxpayer's dinero he could have spent on this shoestring expedition, to date."

Fiona gazed about and even helped him with the nose bags. But she didn't seem to be following his drift. So as they began to water the stock together he gently explained, "He hired you, a green hand, no offense, and even then he tried to get more than his money's worth out of you. The help at the hotel had him down as cheap, too. Yet he'd run up heavy expenses and wired his home office for more. For what? Livery stock hires for two bits a day if you don't ask for any discounts."

She shook her head and said, "These are all government mounts the army post back there provided for the asking, dear."

He nodded grimly and said, "That's worse. His own salary wouldn't have come out of that expense account. What was he paying you, if you'd care to tell me?"

She sighed and said, "A dollar a day. Not that I've seen that much of it, so far. He paid my way out here and naturally paid for all but that last day at the hotel. He also gave me five dollars in advance and said we'd settle up at the end of the month. But to tell you the truth I'd have been embarrassed by this time had I not come West with a modest checking account of my own. Now that you mention it I do believe the government must be into me for at least a few dollars."

He told her he'd make sure she got paid. Then they finished bedding down the ponies and bedded themselves down in his bedroll just as the sunrise was gilding the fluttersome leaves above their bitty clearing.

Down where they were, the light was more green as the day grew brighter. She sort of reminded him of a mermaid as she bounced up and down on top like so, the green light glowing on her firm, bare breasts as if they were doing it on the bottom of some inland sea.

Then he finished in her right, on top, and took first watch as she caught some shut-eye.

They were both experienced trail riders. So there was no need for him to explain the advantages of turning in hungry after a hard night ride. She woke up hungry as a bitch wolf, sooner than she would have, otherwise. She didn't fuss about a cold, late breakfast of canned beans and tomato preserves, washed down with cold black coffee. Longarm drank extra coffee before taking his own flop, knowing he'd have time to catch a few needed winks before the caffeine got a good grip on his brain, and sure enough he managed close to four hours before he popped wide awake again.

He'd have possibly slept longer if Fiona, doubtless getting bored with birdsong and pony farts, hadn't started to blow "Boots and Saddles" on his French horn.

That woke him up all bright-eyed and bushy-tailed and she went at it with him just as wild until they'd come in the orchard grass outside the bedroll, naked as jays by broad-ass daylight with her begging for more. Then, as he lit a smoke, seated back atop the canvas, Fiona began to cry and ask what oh what he must think of her, now that she'd lost her head and committed crimes against nature like one of those

81

shameless pagan Shee figures carved on stone pillars back in the old country and all and all.

He soothed he'd noticed she didn't smoke tobacco and assured her he'd been guilty as anyone in the eyes of many a state morals code, adding, "It's a good thing I'm a federal lawman. I'd have to arrest myself for coming in a pretty lady's pussy in the Bible Belt. Unwed couples ain't allowed to come at all and husbands and wives are required by statute law to wear nightgowns at all times and never touch one another's privates with their bare hands, speaking of crimes against nature. If you want my opinion, a man that concerned about the privates of folk he's never even met has to be sort of queer in his own right."

She moved over to snuggle closer, confiding, "I know I'm wicked and deserve to land in hell, in the end. But, ooh, Custis, when I saw how delicious your rising *srub na gradh* looked . . ."

"I told you I didn't mind you kissing it well," he said. Then, cutting in with a resigned sigh, he pleaded, "Please don't tell me how you got started down the primrose path to perdition, honey. I don't want to hear about other men using and abusing such a pretty little thing. I know it's supposed to inspire men when they hear tell about other men pioneering paradise ahead of 'em to clear all the obstacles to passion but, somehow, it ain't."

She snuggled closer and confided, "I'm sort of curious about where *you* learned to rock the man in the boat so sweetly, as a matter-of-fact."

He said, "I know. I just said women like to talk about it more than men, for all their blushing and shushing. I disremember who first told me how that particular part of she-male anatomy worked. I suspect it was after I'd made more than one neighbor gal come, or say she'd come, the old-fashioned and less skillsome way. Can't we just enjoy each other as pals who just knew how, from the beginning? I met this gal up Montana way who felt like an angel in my arms and really had me talking mushy 'til, for no damn

82

reason at all, she got to telling me how her own father broke her in, perverse as hell, had she been older, and somehow that just ruined my whole evening."

Fiona laughed lewdly and murmured, "Ah, well, I'll not tell you how I was seduced by a well-hung fairy prince who swore he was a frog and my mother never believed he was a frog, either, when she caught us in bed together the next morning."

He laughed, even though he'd heard the joke before, and the rest of their lazy day passed pleasantly enough. They got to play froggy indeed when they found a secluded spring to wallow in that afternoon.

Then they refilled the water bags, supped cold, had each other some more for hot dessert, and were on their way again just after dark. She said at this rate they'd have more fun than trouble retracing the old survey line. He didn't argue. There seemed no profit in both of them feeling this worried as they rode on into the unknown.

Chapter 9

They spent the better part of the night working their way around any possible ambush where the railroad ducked into the Indian Nation through considerable rises. Then they camped before sunrise, caught a few winks along with more beans and grab-ass, and changed to daylight riding for more than one good reason.

Longarm wanted to question angry Choctaw more than he wanted to surprise them in the dark, and Indians' dogs were notorious for barking at strangers from a mile away. After that he wanted to get where they were going. That could be tough enough in broad day.

The rails followed the contour lines of least resistance about fifty miles more or less south through Choctaw country before turning east along the north slopes of the east-west Ouachitas to cut back into Arkansas and scout up more profitable business on the way to Texas if ever it could work its way through the damned mountains. The pass east of Rich Mountain didn't figure in the survey lines, past or future, so Longarm didn't care. He had enough on his plate just herding Fiona and her instruments through country more complex in real life than aboard any damn fool paper map.

The Trail of Tears had been unjust and cruel enough without a heap of bullshit added to the legend by history writers, red or white, who'd never seen either the original or new reserves of the Indians involved. So the legend went that eastern woodland folk of the noble savage persuasion had simply been rounded up by the army at gunpoint and force-marched out to the Great American Desert to starve to death on sun-baked dust dunes.

As ever in the Greek tragedy of the American Indian, things had been a might less simple. To begin with, both the major Muskogee- and Cherokee-speaking bands had sided with the British, or British agents, against their white American neighbors in both the Revolution and the War of 1812. Andrew Jackson had been lashed to a wagon wheel by redcoats and beaten with big black whips as a kid in the Revolution. He was more famous for fighting redcoats, and their Indian allies, as Old Hickory. So despite the way the civilized tribes had taken to behaving by the time Jackson made it to the White House, nobody had been too surprised by his siding with whites, sincerely worried or simply larcenous, against their dusky and likely treacherous Indian neighbors.

General Winfield Scott had been saddled with the chore of moving them out West where they'd likely scare folk less. The Cherokee, making the most fuss about moving, had suffered most as the blue sleeves moved them anyway. The other nations, along with not a few Cherokee, had opted for more quiet passive resistance. A heap had never been rounded up to begin with and still lived in the wooded hills east of the Mississippi, not a few intermarried and accepted as mountain whites a tad more brunette than some. Others had dropped out along the way to settle the same way in the same sort of wooded hills on the Arkansas side of the line. By this late in the game, having way more noble savages

85

to deal with, the B.I.A. seldom fussed at an Indian living off the Great White Father's blanket as long as he or she didn't put in for any government handouts.

Those poor unfortunates who'd allowed themselves to be resettled in the eastern third of the future state of Oklahoma weren't exactly starving to death on the barren dunes of the Great American Desert. Their new Western ranges had been chosen, some said with the help of Thomas Jefferson's Western survey records, with the original homelands of the Southeastern tribes in mind. You had to get west of longitude one hundred degrees, well west of the Indian allotments, before the land refused to support trees away from summer water. The Choctaw Strip along the eastern matches of the Indian Nation, like the Cherokee Strip to the north, was hilly, better than half-timbered, and mighty green for a desert.

It would have been bullshitting the other way to proclaim the Nation green and well-watered as Appalachia, but parts of it got tolerably close and, in truth, such poverty as the transplanted Indians suffered was inflicted upon them by flatland slickers, if not their own lack of book-learning.

Longarm told, or warned, Fiona they'd find a mean white or shiftless Indians behind any serious deprivation in such easygoing country. The government had set aside a prodigious amount of land for the numbers of mouths to be fed. All the civilized tribes knew how to farm and the soil was tolerable where it was halfway flat bottomland. But of course, as in the case of the twice-over mountain whites on the other side of the survey line, a man too shiftless to plant some beans and corn, gather hickory nuts and wild game from the hardwoods all about, or drop a line in the nearest creek for a catfish fry just had to do without and the Indians, at least, got regular government handouts lest they all got to beating drums and making faces at more nervous folk.

Fiona remained unconvinced about Indians living whiter than some trash whites who had to support themselves entire, even though they passed a distant cabin, now and again, that Dan'l Boone might have felt right at home in.

He told her Sam Houston, dwelling amid the Cherokee of the West as their agent that time, had hired Cherokee carpenters to build him a log mansion the Boones never could have afforded. She said she'd heard they'd had their own schoolhouses and published their own newspapers but wonder if it counted, reading and writing in Indian tongues. He said he figured it did, adding, "*We* got book learning from the ancient Greeks and Romans. The Good Book was writ first in Hebrew, then Greek, then Latin, before King James said he'd rather read it in English. Are you saying England is uncivilized?"

She laughed and told him that had been the wrong question to ask an Irish gal who preferred her *own* Good Books in Latin. She asked if it was true the great Indian educator, Sequoia, had never learned to speak English. He said he didn't know, asked her if King James had spoken Hebrew and opined it was to Sequoia's credit if he'd figured out his alphabet for the Cherokee lingo with no help at all from any white teachers.

They'd been treading through second growth and hence thick loblolly with the pine needles high and low on all sides as they were settling up on Sequoia. So Longarm smelled the trouble ahead before he could see a blamed thing. He swore softly and waved Fiona and her own pack brutes up closer before he told her, quietly, "Don't peer about or make argumentative gestures no matter how odd you may feel I'm acting. We've strayed farther up this slope from the railroad right-of-way than I'd have allowed for, had I smelled what I'm smelling right now a mite sooner."

Fiona sniffed, twice, and decided, "Poteen. We had neighbors from the old country who made their own creature comforts no matter what Protestant tax collectors say about revenue stamps and all and all."

Longarm muttered, "Not so loud. I ain't sure how you make the Irish brand of white lightning. Someone around

87

here boils his corn mash with sorghum molasses. Indians ain't supposed to even *drink* firewater, let alone *distill* it, smack on a reservation."

She gulped and asked, "Do you really have to arrest them and all and all?"

To which he replied with an honest chuckle, "I could try. I doubt I could carry even one back to Fort Smith without getting us both shot in the back more than once. But I don't ride for the revenue service, thank God, and even if I did I don't have a warrant to serve on anyone in these parts."

She said she was glad and suggested they simply ride on. He sighed and said, "If we know they're cooking mash in these woods they know we know it and so now they're waiting to see what we do next."

She asked what one did next when one stumbled on a hidden still in thick pine. He said, "Act neighborly about it, of course. Let me take the lead again. Then tag along after me, acting as if we stumble over stills all the time and never get excited."

She gulped and said she'd try. Hoping she'd be taken for a boy in her tight jeans and loose shirt, with her hair back inside her high-crowned Stetson, Longarm heeled the paint he'd been riding on, sniffing about until, sure enough, he spotted the squat homegrown whisky operation up through the trees to their left.

He turned toward it. Fiona, bless her, followed without comment. There was naturally not a soul in sight as he dismounted at the edge of the clearing, about thirty yards across, and strode over afoot, not looking around as he reached the scene of the crime. They were cooking, not distilling, yet. The sweet and sour smelling mixture of rough-ground corn and sorghum squeezings had to be boiled to a total mush, then cooled and allowed to ferment a spell before the next step. So it was safe to ignore the pot still and copper coil just the other side of the wood pile. Longarm found a gourd scoop, dipped a little mash out of the simmering cauldron, and sniffed the results knowingly before he tossed it back in, set the gourd back where he'd found it, and shoved a couple of yard-long lengths of split pine into the hot coals under the cooking mash before he strode back to Fiona and the ponies to remount and mutter, "Let's drift on. It ought to be safe enough, now."

It was. Not a bird made one peep from the pines all about as they rode casually away, trending downslope toward the railroad tracks until they spied them through the trees ahead. They burst out of the trees on a dirt service road alongside the tracks. Fiona moved up beside Longarm to demand some explanation of his grotesque behavior back there, as she put it.

He said, "I wasn't being grotesque, I was aiding and abetting. Lord knows how many Choctaw moonshiners might have been watching as I tested their mash and put more firewood under it, like the neighborly stranger I wanted them to feel I was."

She smiled uncertainly and said, "In Connemara it's not considered wise for a stranger to go anywhere near such a private operation."

He shrugged and said, "This ain't Connemara. Moonshiners in these parts, red or white, know you can't witness against anyone you've aided and abetted unless you'd like to go to jail along *with* 'em. I know they didn't think they needed my modest help back yonder. They knew it, too. What I was telling 'em, at a safe, silent distance for all concerned, was that we weren't revenuers and savvied the rules of polite society in these hills."

She grimaced and said, "I was afraid you were about to get us both massacred by wild Indians back there. Do you think they're really going to drink all that poteen themselves?"

He laughed and replied, "Not hardly. The Cherokee get most of their corn liquor from a white trash moonshiner called Miss Belle, up to Younger's Bend on the Arkansas. You know about as much as me about conditions here in the Choctaw Strip. Like I said, Choctaw don't have as much to say to our kind. It's the Indians who carry on you read most about in the papers. That's doubtless why Lakota are more famous than Comanche when, pound for pound, the Comanche have killed way more, red and white, than all the other horse Indians put together."

She sighed and said, "I wish you could tell me more about Choctaw. I know it was their tribal council who complained about missing bench marks but Captain Boyle said something about savage superstitions and the idea some trees could be haunted by evil spirits and all and all."

Longarm knew a thing or two about savage superstitions. So he weighed the notions some before he shrugged and said, "I hear tell most of the white hill folk in the Ouachitas set great store by the Pentecostal or Holy Rolling Movement. Don't know whether Pentecostal preachers hold with wood sprites. Thought it was the Druids, back in the old countries, who worried most about that. The Quapaw erect peeled saplings where an important Quapaw's died and decorate it sort of like a Christmas tree. The civilized tribes all set store by council trees to meet under or witness trees to mark off boundaries. Never heard of any Indian saying a particular tree was haunted, though. Even if they did, would Indians cutting down haunted trees complain to the B.I.A. about it?"

She said, "Some white settlers have complained about missing bench marks they'd based their homestead claims on, you know."

Longarm shrugged and said, "Most of the whites in the Ouachitas are still hardscrabble squatters. It was mostly formal complaints from the Choctaw council and their white agent as inspired all this government concern. But I'll keep Indian malcontents or Druids a long way from home in mind. Now let's get some riding in."

They did. By noon they'd covered many a mile over a rolling patchwork of old or new growth timber and cleared grassland dotted with old stumps and newer cows, mostly Texican longhorns, with not so many cut for steer beef as one might have seen on Mex- or Anglo-managed range. Aside from growing up tougher to begin with, young bullocks could fuss off an awesome amount of beef, figuring out who the herd bull might be.

The Choctaw had plenty of pork ranging free in the hardwoods as well. The razorback hog was not native to the hickory or beech groves of North America. That may have been what made them such wild animals when one encountered 'em in the second growth they favored, east or west of the Mississippi. But Longarm didn't shoot to kill the few times they were bluff-charged by old, gnashy sows with chipmunk-striped young rooting after 'em. He explained to Fiona how a stranger who had to kill a mean root hog was still supposed to deliver it to its owner, cleaned and dressed for smoking.

When it got fly-biting hot he called a halt where the railroad service road forded a purling stream in the shade of the rail trestle and peach-leaved willow, alder, and sycamore, with some green simmon and slippery elm, untouched, to indicate few Indian boys or hoboes knew the shady draw. But after they'd watered their stock, when Fiona began to unbutton her shirt, Longarm warned, "Too close to the railroad for skinny dipping, kitten. We'd best move on up a bend or more, soon as these thirsty critters settle down."

She asked if they could risk a fire as well as a skinny dip. He started to say yes. They were well clear of Fort Smith by now with no indication they'd been followed. They meant to openly contact the Choctaw once they made Poteau Junction that very sundown at the rate they were going. He still said, "Best not and say we did. They got a big old trading post just a spit and a holler from here and I'll be proud to buy you a sit-down supper with half-moon pie and fresh-perked Arbuckle coffee once we see we have the settlement to ourselves and the regular inhabitants."

She sighed and said, "Pooh, who'd be after us this far from Fort Smith and all and all?"

He cocked an eyebrow her way and declared, "Same person or persons unknown who backshot Boyle, of course.

They never killed him to keep him from running a survey of Fort Smith, and anyone opposed to a survey of the infernal Ouachitas has to know we have to get to them to survey 'em, right?"

She didn't argue further. He dismounted to lead the whole shebang upstream and around some willows and cottonwood on foot. Once he had, even Fiona was glad. They'd come upon an even nicer site for forty winks or, as she suggested, a friendly fondle in knee-deep and still-green love grass, so-called because stock just loved to eat it and it smelled mighty romantic to humankind. Longarm tethered the six ponies where they could get at both the cool grass and sweet water. Then he moved on up to the far side of the modest clearing with Fiona, his Winchester, and her bedroll. As she helped him spread the bedding out across the love grass, kneeling beside him, she laughed like a mean little kid and opined they had this little Eden all to themselves, like Adam and Eve before the fall.

Longarm sighed and told her she was wrong, adding, "Don't look this way but there's a buck Indian regarding us from that alder clump just up and across the creek from here. He's good, even allowing this is his country and he could make an educated guess where we'd hole up to siesta as the day heated up."

Fiona moaned, "Mother of God and what do we do now?"

He said, "We're doing it. He knows that I've spotted him. It's way harder to spot an Indian when he don't want you to spot him. He's just waiting to see how trigger-happy we may be before he moves into point-blank pistol range. Must be one of the boys we helped cook mash, back yonder. Doubt anyone else would expose himself so subtle."

She asked what on earth the young Indian could want. Longarm said, "We'll find out when they get around to telling us. You're right about how young he is. You get to be an older, more important Indian by letting the kids have all the glory."

They'd finished spreading her bedding across the grass. He told her to keep her shirt on and they stretched out atop the canvas cover side by side, the Winchester across the foot of the bedroll. He fished out a cheroot and lit up. That seemed the signal the Choctaw had been watching for. The young one staring poker-faced from that clump of alders across the way was suddenly simply no longer there. Fiona gulped and murmured, "Custis, behind you, coming down from further up the slope!"

So Longarm sat back up, casually turning his head enough to make out a short, paunchy individual of about forty, coming their way in bib overalls and a straw hat, with his black hair braided with scarlet ribbons.

Longarm broke out another cheroot. The stocky Indian stopped a few paces away and gravely declared, "I am not here to beg for tobacco. I am rich as well as beautiful. You can call me Possom Dancing. Would you like to tell me who you are, and why those other white boys have been following you?"

Longarm gravely puffed his cheroot a time or two, studied the tip as if he'd never noticed how tobacco burned before, and replied, "I am U.S. Deputy Custis Long. This here is Miss Fiona Coyne of the U.S. Survey Service. We have come because our Choctaw brothers asked us to look at your borders through the Ouachitas to the south. Have you heard about the funny business down that way?"

Possom Dancing squatted down, replying, "I do not think it is funny to cut down a witness tree. It is worse to mark another tree as if it was the same one. I think a man who would do that would mark another man's cow with his own brand. Who did you say those other white boys were?"

Longarm said, "We wasn't sure they were following us until just now. How many of 'em and what makes you so certain they were following us and not just passing through?"

The Choctaw said, "There were three of them. All white men wearing dusty black suits. One wore a straw planter's hat. The other two wore wool hats, like you. They passed us closer to the tracks. So they did not see us. We saw they were scouting for signs as they rode, slower than travelers in a hurry. Faster than riders with plenty of time to work with. I think they rode on into the junction. That is a good place to ask about others who may have gone before. That is a good place to wait for someone who hasn't ridden that far through the Nation yet. Forget what they say about that settlement called Rome. All trails lead through Poteau Junction in *this* neck of the woods!"

Longarm puffed on his cheroot and silently held the other out to the older man. When the Indian took it with a barely noticeable nod Longarm told Fiona, "I'd best go on in, alone, and see what they want. You'll be safer here. Now that we know where everyone sets on the board you may as well build a campfire and start a decent pot of jerky stew. I ought to be back to help you eat it by the time it's fit to eat."

She protested, "You can't ride in alone against three gun hands who'll be expecting you, from cover they've had plenty of time to choose, Custis!"

The Indian finished lighting his own smoke before he softly said, "They told us one of the government riders they were sending in might be Custis Long, the one better known as Longarm. Could that be who those other strangers seem to be after?"

Longarm modestly allowed the shrewd-eyed Indian was correct in his assumption. Possom Dancing inhaled deeply and proclaimed, "I think this tobacco has good medicine after all. We have heard of the good work Longarm has done in other parts of the Nation. I would not trust a Cherokee's word on the time if we were both staring at the same clock. But the South Cheyenne and Osage say Longarm knows what he is doing and for all their faults neither Those Who Cut Fingers nor Those Who Slash Throats lie half as much as Cherokee."

Fiona didn't look convinced yet. Longarm said, "I told you before I was figuring on sundown with this siesta thrown in. Do I saddle back up and push on through the high noon heat I can likely get in and get back by sundown, see?"

She sniffed and demanded, "What's to become of me, out here in these lonesome woods, in the meantime?"

It would have been more awkward for Longarm. So he was grateful when Possom Dancing snorted in disgust and said, "Can't you see us smoking together, you foolish girl? Do you think you'd have seen us at all if we meant harm to either of you? I just told you we were hoping Longarm would come and do something about the complaints of our own council. Do you really think we would risk the red thoughts of Longarm and our Choctaw elders, just for a piece of ass! Hear me, you must think your ass is worth many ponies!"

Fiona laughed despite herself and all three of them had to laugh when she demurely replied she'd had few complaints. Then, that settled, Possom Dancing said, "I have some cooking of my own to attend. But I will have someone with less to do posted up above with a cleared view of the rails and trails to and from the junction."

As Longarm nodded and got to his feet the older Indian, rising at the same time, added, "I would send some of my boys in with you if there were more of us. Right now I can keep an eye on your woman and other good things, here. But that is all and she is right about there being three of them. What she said about them having time to set up a good ambush if they are expecting you makes sense, too. Why don't you wait 'til I can send a runner over the mountain to gather more help? I could put together a nice posse by nightfall."

Longarm said, "I was hoping to settle up and be back here by then. I got my own advantages, now, thanks to you. They've no way of knowing I might know they know I'm coming, see?"

Fiona got to her feet as well, protesting, "We *don't* see, Custis. What's the big hurry? Why not do it Mr. Dancing's way, the safe way?"

95

Longarm shook his head and said, "I told you before about telegraph wires and railroad trains. I want to hit 'em before the afternoon southbound gets here, just in case, and a sissy who did every fool thing the safe way wouldn't be here in the first place, right?"

Chapter 10

Longarm had noticed along the trail that the late Captain Boyle's big army bay had a long stride as well as a vague description at any distance. As he was cinching his McClellan aboard it Possom Dancer mentioned a moonshiner's trail few strangers, red or white, ought to know about. He didn't have to explain why anyone cooking mash north of town might want to pack his finished product in from the south. He told Longarm, "If I wanted to ambush anyone around Poteau Junction and had plenty of time to count the ways I think I'd settle on the hayloft of the Tenkiller Livery across from the railroad platform. From up there I'd command both the railroad service road and the north-south post road. I'd expect most anyone riding in to visit the general store across the way, cattywise, and best of all I'd know there was only the Widow Tenkiller and her colored help to stop me."

Longarm knew Tenkiller was a Cherokee name. So he didn't ask why a widow by that name with no Choctaw backing might have less than most to say about the uses or abuses of her hayloft. He thanked the older man for the advice, shook with Fiona lest the Indians watching them think he was mushy, and lit out for the town an hour's ride or more away.

The day was shaping up a real brain frier, even riding through dappled shade along the moonshiner's zigzag through loblolly and hardwoods, mostly oak, gum, and shagbark on the sunnier slopes with black locust, alder, and sycamore choking the many gullies the sneaky trail followed oft as possible.

He paused in a shady but still sweaty dell to rest his mount and change into a fresh shirt and clean, dry jeans. He did so mostly for comfort. He knew a white rider was sure to stand out and attract a certain amount of gossip no matter how he might dress or behave his fool self. For in the Indian Nation even the law was supposed to be Indian, now that President Hayes had forgiven those bands who'd sided with the Confederacy that time.

Longarm naturally packed some of those blank arrest warrants a white federal deputy might need in these parts, stating the son of a bitch he was after was "a white or black man and not an Indian by birth, marriage, or adoption into any tribe."

The Indian Police knew as well as anyone that there were outlaws with no use at all for Indians who found it best to call themselves breeds or get some Indian drunk to marry or adopt 'em. The poorly armed and self-trained Indian Police did their best, but some had different views as to just what constituted a crime. They could crack down hard on anyone red, black, or white who violated their own notions of decency. But Longarm preferred to work alone in a country where a man who screwed a distant cousin was more likely to hang than a horse thief. Longarm knew many an Indian felt he or she had more in common with a stranger who'd been outlawed by the government than he might with the government who'd pushed him and his kind around for no good reason he could see.

Longarm dismounted in an alder hell south of the junction, nose-bagged the captain's bay, and eased into town from the south, hugging the tree line with his Winchester cradled casual over one shirtsleeve. There wasn't too much scouting called for in a settlement of less than a thousand souls when the church bells were ringing. The rail lines from the north and northeast merging there on the shores of the so-called Poteau River called for more railroad installations than Indian Agency construction. The Choctaw, like other farmers, stockmen, or moonshiners, preferred to dwell more spread out. So there were only a few private homes to work around as Longarm made for the cluster of business buildings around the railroad water tower and church steeple.

Albeit listed as one of the five civilized tribes and granted their own constitution 'til they'd blown it by siding with the losing side in the war, the Choctaw, like other Creek speakers, hadn't taken up as many sharp tactics from the whites as say the Cherokee. So it came as no surprise to Longarm when he saw the general store was run by colored folk and that the railroad workers lounging on the open platform across from that livery Possom Dancing had mentioned seemed white as he was. He worked his way around to the back of the barn-like but unpainted frame livery to roll through some corral rails and make it across some ass-puckering open ground to the cooler straw-scented shade with his carbine held port arms but aimed polite.

He still seemed to have scared a colored kid with a manure fork half to death. Before the stable hand could stick him with the shitty tines Longarm snapped, "I'm the law. How many other white men on the premises and don't lie."

The stable hand seemed sincere as he replied in a tone of confusion that Longarm was the first white man he'd seen in here for some time.

They were still working on that when a chunky built but sort of pretty woman in a print Mother Hubbard came back from the occupied stalls, up front, to ask what was going on.

Longarm repeated he was the law, in search of three white men in black who just might be up in her hayloft. The pleasantly moon-faced Indian woman, really a girl at second glance, said she was the Widow Tenkiller and that she didn't have any white men in her hayloft, as far as she knew.

Longarm asked if she'd get sore if he looked. She told him to go right ahead. He never asked her to climb the ladder after him, but when she did he helped her up the last few rungs, once he'd swept the half-empty hayloft with his eyes and gun muzzle. He saw they had more time to jaw than they would have, the other way, and filled her in a mite as he eased over to the open hay hatch with his Winchester to see Possom Dancing had been on the money about ambushing anyone riding in from the north less careful. The high vantage point offered a clear shot at most anyone along the one main street down yonder. The Indian girl, who said her pals called her Rosie, said she knew about those three white riders. They'd called on her earlier that same afternoon, asking if she'd seen any white riders. They hadn't described anyone they were after. They'd neglected to tell her why. She said they'd bought some supplies across the way and lit out south, likely anxious to make it to Page that same evening.

Longarm squinted his eyes as he pictured his mental map of these parts. Once he had he shook his head dubiously and said, "That'd be a fair ride on a mighty hot day if we're talking about that last rail stop before the tracks swing west along the north slope of the Ouachitas, Miss Rosie."

She shrugged and said, "It's less than thirty miles and they seemed interested in the powwow down yonder when I mentioned it."

Longarm asked her to mention it to him. She said. "They asked if any of our Indian Police were here in town this afternoon. When I told 'em most every important Choctaw in these parts had gone down to Page to powwow about those white trash cutting down their witness trees two of 'em

100

agreed they'd doubtless find the folk they were after down around Page. One of 'em argued they ought to tarry here a spell because he was sure they'd been making better time. He was outvoted, though, as anyone can plainly see from here. There's not a strange mount anywhere in sight."

Longarm started to reach absently for a cheroot, remembered where he was, and muttered, "I have a strange mount, tethered out of sight an easy walk from here. That one who voted to wait here in this junction knew what he was talking about. He might have gone on arguing, more convincing, and if they double back this is still the best place to lay for me, if I wasn't already up here, I mean."

She seemed to savvy what he meant. She asked him to describe his own pony and give her a grander notion where it might be found. Once he had she moved over to the ladderway and called down to her young hand.

He called back up that he'd be proud to go fetch Longarm's mount and lead it in the back way for a rubdown and some cracked corn. She told him to make sure nobody saw him doing it. Longarm seconded the motion. Then they had the whole place to themselves for a spell. As they got better acquainted, over by the hay hatch, it developed she was Chickasaw by birth and more recently Cherokee by marriage. Her man had been killed in the corral out back, trying to bust an outlaw pony that had busted his neck, instead. She didn't have to tell him why she had so few social callers, trying to run the business by herself the past two years. Possom Dancing had already told him the Tenkiller Livery was a lonesome lookout when one considered how close it was to the center of town.

Longarm told her more about his own reasons for existence in her neck of the woods. He didn't leave out the part about the government surveyor he was guarding, nor, when asked, that Miss Coyne was young and pretty enough. But when the Indian widow asked whether he and that white gal were lovers he chided, "That's betwixt me and her, Miss Rosie. How would you like it if I was to kiss and tell on you like a sniggersome kid who still picks at his fool face?"

She sighed and soberly said, "At least I could say I'd been kissed. You've no idea how these shiftless Creek hate anyone with a head for business, Custis. While he was alive, and paying for the drinks, my man seemed to be admired as a good old boy, Cherokee or not, and he never cheated anyone around here, damn their jealous remarks!"

He assured her he'd met honest Cherokee in his wide travels. He wasn't sure how you told a lady to get the hell out of her own hayloft so's a man could pay attention to the scene below. He was hunkered on the bare planking the forkers had stood on to fork hay back under the eaves, of course. It was her hay as well as her hayloft. So he had no call to object when she commenced to haul armfuls of sweet-cured timothy and blue stem over to spread near the hatch as a softer set-down. When she invited him to, and set her own chunky self down beside him, he had to allow it felt nicer lying prone with his gun sights trained over the splintery edge.

He had no call to aim at the railroad workers across the way or the colored lady sweeping her store steps. As the lazy afternoon got ever warmer everyone ducked out of sight and he had even less to study on down yonder. Up where he lay in wait for whatever, the Widow Tenkiller kept buzzing in his ear like a bluebottle fly against a shithouse window. She sure had a lot of complaints stored up about her Choctaw neighbors, albeit, as far as he cared to hear they'd mostly just dealt with her fair in business and left her alone social. He could see how that might leave a healthy young gal feeling starved for social contacts. But when she commenced to promise him a grand set-down supper and a swell breakfast as well, if he wanted, Longarm felt obliged to tell her he'd promised he'd be back to sup with others, out in the woods, around sundown.

She protested the afternoon was already half-shot and asked how he ever meant to spy those other riders if he lit out before they could get back.

He explained, "The longer I gaze down through that heat shimmer the less I expect to, Miss Rosie. Nobody with a lick of sense rides fast or far on an afternoon hot as this one if there's any cooler shade to set in. I suspected they might double back to lay for me here once they failed to cut any sign on the trail to the south. But as you see, they ain't. I reckon they've given me credit for covering my tracks and pushing on to that big Choctaw powwow."

He shifted his weight on the straw, suppressing a yawn, and decided, "I'll hold on 'til three or so. You just never know 'til you make sure. They're doubtless searching for some deep shade to stay put in 'til then, even as we speak."

The Widow Tenkiller sighed and said, "I wish you weren't in such an all-fired hurry to leave. I've always been sort of shy around men."

Then she rolled to her knees to simply shuck her loose-fitting Mother Hubbard up over her head, spread the thin cotton neatly on the straw and flop buck-naked by his side, her moon face blushed a duskier shade and her firm tawny flesh aglow with desire to please and be pleased.

Longarm gulped and lay flatter on his belly, hoping his own feelings might not show, through his soft denim jeans, as he murmured, "That's awfully flattering, Miss Rosie. Temptin' as well, if I didn't have three riders and your own stable hand to worry about."

She snuggled closer, soothing, "You can see out just as well with your own stuffy things off and just let *me* worry about my hired hands. I've noticed before this how nice it feels to lie naked in this cross-breezed loft on a hot day. They know better than to pester me when I'm up here alone or entertaining company."

He gulped and said he'd just worry about those three riders, in that case, trying to get flatter on his gut lest she notice the way he was rising to the occasion inside his soft denim jeans.

It wasn't fair. Gals could pretend they didn't want to, or vice versa, while a man's true feelings tended to show. He asked if it didn't embarrass her, lying jay naked near the gaping hay hatch in broad-ass daylight. She said, "Pooh, we're on the shady side and higher than anything across the way but yon water tower. Do you see anybody peeking at us from the water tower?"

He had to allow he didn't as, by this time, she was tugging at the gun rig around his hips and begging to get at the buckle. He laughed, got rid of his hat while he was at it, but warned her he was a tumbleweed rider inclined to love and leave ladies in the lurch, mean as it sounded.

She moaned, "Damn it, I don't want to get engaged. I want to get laid! I haven't had any for close to a year and . . ."

"Say no more and let's see what we can do for what ails you, ma'am," he cut in, laying his Winchester aside, albeit handy, as he gathered the chunky love-starved widow in for some down-home satisfaction. He found her mighty satisfying, too, once they'd come together sort of frantic, then gotten him undressed all the way, as well, to treat her right, Indian style.

Like most members of the civilized tribes, Rosie knew how to make love the same as other Christians were supposed to. But thanks to some time spent in wilder surroundings with more old-fashioned members of her race, Longarm suspected she'd admire that puppy dog panting and licking at her gaping mouth as inspiring as some white gals found French-kissing. It made her moan and croon sweet things at him in her own melodious lingo while her love-starved innards rippled the length of his questing manhood in a milking motion that might have kept a dead man hard, and humping. She took it as a grand compliment when she felt him ejaculate deep inside her and then keep going. When she told him he was a credit to his race he assured her she was a credit to her own and the nice thing was that they both meant it.

Later, sharing a smoke as they cooled their flushed flesh in the gentle cross-ventilation of the sweet-smelling hayloft, they agreed what they'd just done was one of the few human enterprises where honest emotion and selfish pleasure-seeking improved the relationship. She said that to be perfectly honest she wanted to get on top. So he let her and again he had to agree there was a lot to be said for greedy hogwallow lust, on her part, at least. He had to keep one eye peeled for less friendly riding, down below.

But whilst honest emotion had its place in the ways of a man with a maid, no man with a lick of sense told one woman he'd been in another the very same day unless all parties concerned were mighty good pals. So, Fiona and Rosie not even knowing each other, Longarm tried to save a polite amount of passion for later and, again, Rosie took the time he was taking in her as a compliment. So bewixt one damned thing and another, the following sunrise caught him and Fiona on the trail, way this side of that big powwow at the jerkwater stop and post office called Page.

Longarm wasn't about to ride in from the north with such a pretty she-male target as an added bonus. So he started gazing about for a safe place to cache Fiona and such stock and gear as he might not want in his way in a gunfight.

Fiona wanted to camp some more in some woods, so he could relieve the itch she'd acquired riding astride half the night in thin jeans, she said. He said he'd have been proud to scratch her crotch for her some more in virgin timber if there'd been any handy, this close to irrigation ditches running north from the Ouachita foothills. But Page was more famous for the homesteads around it than its own modest size. All the bottomland they kept passing seemed to have been plowed up for the Indian trilogy of corn, squash, and beans where they hadn't drilled in cash crops of tobacco or sorghum.

The half-agricultural woodland culture the five civilized tribes had invented the other side of civilization offered somewhat less profit but called for way less field work than farming white style. The corn, squash, and beans grew together so's the big leaves of the squash vines planted between the corn stalks could smother most unwanted weeds.

The bean vines planted in the same hills as the seed corn fertilized the roots of the very corn stalks they wound up, saving the Indians the bother of bean poles and not hurting the corn crop half as much as white settlers held.

Tobacco sold best if it was grown and cured the white planter's way and of course the Indians had learned about sorghum or Chinese sugarcane from their white neighbors as well. So even though it was distant kin to American corn, with its value more in its fleshy stalk than in its punier seed heads, they grew sorghum in tidy cultivated rows and let it have more sun and water to fatten on.

There were more slopes than bottomlands, this close to the mountains to the south, of course, and some mayhaps overly civilized tribesmen had put browsing black goats in with their calico longhorns to keep second growth saplings from getting a fair start on the mostly logged-off range. Fiona spied a distant cottonwood grove she pronounced a great place to have a lie-down. Longarm pointed at blue chimney smoke in the same general direction and told her, "I got a better notion. Instead of getting caught as trespassers on posted range, what say we ride in polite and offer to pay for such favors as we might ask?"

So that was how he cached Fiona and all but the paint pony he decided to ride the rest of the way into Page.

The elderly couple dwelling childless but well-provided with pigs and chickens in a tidy, boxed-in dogtrot house with a turkey-feather-shingled roof looked colored to Fiona. Longarm felt no call to dispute their claim to membership in at least one of the five civilized tribes. The motherly old lady said they were just in time for breakfast, late as it really was, and the old man told Longarm not to talk dirty when he mentioned paying them to let Fiona and the other ponies stay there for a spell.

He knew they'd feel even more insulted if he rode on without even tasting an old woman's cooking. So he truthfully enjoyed some pork sausages and corn fritters on the porch with Fiona and the old man, who allowed he always had room for one more serving slathered in genuine berry patch honey.

Fiona simply enjoyed it. Longarm knew enough about Indians to be curious about the clear golden honey served from a mason jar. He knew that while the white race owed a heap of crops to the American Indian while the latter had adopted a heap of white notions in turn, keeping bees and producing honey this fine wasn't one of them. No Indian had ever seen the old world honey bee before the whites had brought them across the main ocean. So even those Indians who'd learned to raid wild beehives for a fair enough mishmash of honey, wax, and bee parts tended to think of honey bees as "white men's flies."

The old couple confirmed his suspicion the stuff had been store-bought when he mentioned how pure it poured. The old man said they sold it, cheap, in Page. Some white settler kept bees just up the rail line on the Arkansas side of the line. Fiona was more interested in anyone, on either side of the line, who might have a motive for shifting said line. As the old lady served more corn fritters and the odd notion some Indians seemed to have about coffee, her husband said he'd heard about the trouble up along Rich Mountain Ridge. He said the Choctaw Police and some of the tribal elders were holding a council about it at this very time. He had no suggestions to offer on who might be cutting down witness trees and shifting the old bench marks to new ones. He agreed it seemed a dumb way to grab land, as soon as one studied on it. Waving his old dark claw expansively at that cottonwood grove Fiona had wanted to get laid in, the old-timer said, "I used to have a witness tree in yonder grove. It got lightning struck and rotted out years ago. Don't matter. We got this 'lotment platted on the B.I.A. claims chart and, aside from that, we got *bones* buried on this land."

His old woman looked away but confirmed in a small, choked-up voice, "Four of our little ones as never 'mounted to much and an eldest boy stampeded to death over on the Chisholm Trail just before his nineteenth birthday."

Her husband nodded soberly and said, "We raised eight more to men and women grown, praise the Lord, and be that as it may, there's still no way you can grab land, permanent, just by shifting an old bench mark. You might get away with it a season or so. But sooner or later someone's bound to notice, demand a new survey, and *then* where are you for all your slickery?"

Longarm had no answer to offer. The old folk dwelt better than an hour by train or a day by buckboard from the disputed survey line, and true Choctaw or peckerwood whites were apt to know more about any dispute to begin with. So he finished his coffee and allowed he'd best ride into Page, the long way 'round as well as lonesome, and see if anyone there might know.

As he was changing his McClellan to a less jaded cordovan barb Fiona repeated her objections to being left behind. She intimated he was only leaving her behind because he thought she was a sissy girl who didn't know how to fight. She said, "I can handle a gun good as most men. I used to go hunting with my dad and uncles and if I were to cover your back as you scouted for those strangers who've been dogging us . . ."

"We'd have nobody covering *your* back," he cut in. "I'd as soon scout alone if you were an ugly boy, kitten. I could tell you a tale of James Butler Hickok gunning his own deputy in a tense situation, but suffice it to say I'd just as soon not have to worry about anyone but me in a shootout in strange surroundings. I mean to pussyfoot in and contemplate the scene from cover before I pay any courtesy calls on the Indian police. As soon as I see it's safe there for the both of us I'll come back for you. It ain't that far so it shouldn't take that long."

She asked, "What if you don't come back? What if you get yourself killed?"

He could only reply with a sheepish smile, "You can say you told me so, and I promise I won't argue back."

Chapter 11

Longarm crossed the tracks a mile northwest of Page so he could ride in downhill, through second growth tanglewood, from due south. He dismounted on the far side of a cornfield to tether his mount to a split chestnut rail of the snake fence around the tall corn. Then he strode in along the west side of the wagon trace, hugging the shade of a blackjack and cottonwood windbreak planted there to soften the prevailing squall lines. He passed the bitty cabin that likely went with all that corn, squash, and such. Some chickens clucked out at him in passing but it appeared the folk who lived there had even taken their yard dogs into town with 'em.

As he eased in on what was normally a hamlet of mayhaps a hundred souls, he suspected he could have entered aboard an elephant proceeded by a brass band for all the mostly Indian crowd of at least a thousand might have noticed. Word of any powwow tended to gather folk from near and far and the Choctaw Council was said to be really angry about that bullshit with their border to the east.

Longarm spent some time staring out from a gloomy gap between two buildings, both originally log but now "boxed" with vertical planks to keep winter winds outside where they dammit belonged. Both seemed to be shops set up to face the dirt market street and railroad right-of-way. The one to his left had been whitewashed. The one to his right had been left to weather to a natural silvery gray. That meant Choctaw to the right of him and white or colored to the left of him. At the moment he was more interested in others who might not belong there as a rule.

But as soon as he studied on that he saw hardly anyone in sight seemed a townie, unless the regular residents of the dinky railroad town ran the handful of businesses dressed rustic for a Texas trail drive. Mex and Anglo stockmen had by now evolved a sort of uniform whilst even sod-busting whites tended to gussy up for town as if they wanted to be mistaken for cowhands who'd just been paid. Assimilated Indians could be as original as to costume as they could about house paint. It wasn't true they never painted their houses. They simply never painted 'em white or any other sedate tone. Whitewash was a B.I.A. handout to be scorned. "Too proud to whitewash and too poor to paint" was the way most reservation Indians justified their silvery gray siding. Those who felt the need to show off usually started with fire engine red, hoping for a more dramatic trim.

Such tastes in store-bought notions extended to the go-to-powwow costumes on display this sunny afternoon. Before white contact, the five civilized tribes of the southeastern woodlands had worn well-tailored deer hide, seldom fringed, and colorful striped cloth, spun, dyed and woven from native cotton, most any color one could think of. Left to their own devices, the Choctaw hadn't worn feather bonnets. But now that they were out in the wild West some of the younger cowhands had dyed feathers stuck in the bands of their Texas-crowned Stetsons. The Indian women and girls lollygagging up and down the dirt street as if it was some

110

boulevard in Paris Town were dressed more the way they might have been in olden times, albeit Longarm noticed with just a tad of wistfulness, that most of the gals had sewn their traditional costumes, a sort of cross betwixt Navajo and Gypsy, from store-bought calico that looked somehow wilder than the thicker, softer homespun that was dyed only in simple stripes or bands. The effect was lost, total, when a hefty gal pleated show-off yards of an orange and purple floral print around her fool hips.

Most of the men and boys favored denim or whipcord pants, sober enough hats and boots, save for feathers and jingle bells, and let their loud shirts express any reservations they felt toward Victorian morality and the Pentecostal Movement gaining so much headway among their white neighbors.

Longarm could take his holy rolling with a polite pinch of salt. He knew most Muskogee speakers had been practicing Christians before the religious revivals of the first half of the century had gotten everyone to acting so noisy in church. He knew that despite their dusky features and colorful costumes the five civilized tribes had been more literate and better educated than many of the whites who'd had to be protected from them. A heap of folk passing his look-out, men, women, and children, were likely more closely related to a heap of folk who feared them than either side let on. Like their Muskogee cousins and Cherokee enemies, the Choctaw were matrilineal, counting descent from their mother's side. So to their way of thinking any-one with a Choctaw mother was a Choctaw, red, white, or black as the results might appear. It sure might made the Indian Nation a swell place for big fibbers to hide out.

But Longarm wasn't scouting for outlaws claiming to be Indians, as far as he knew. So he lit a cheroot, stepped out of his slot far enough for an amiable-looking young Choctaw to notice him, and said, "Howdy. I'm looking for the law, hereabouts."

111

The Indian, a vision in blue denim and scarlet sateen, politely asked whether they were talking about the Indian Police or the real Tustenegee.

Longarm replied, "Tustenegee?" with a thoughtful frown.

The young Choctaw nodded a tad smugly and said, "I thought you might be one of them. *Tustenegee* means something like heap big chief only that ain't it. Do I have to tell you what Indian Police are?"

Longarm smiled thinly and said he'd likely make out better with one of them than someone who might not be it. So the Choctaw directed him to that false front down the way with the barber pole out front. He didn't have to explain the door next to the barber shop was the one Longarm wanted. The white lawman took a thoughtful look up and down the street, saw neither that white planter's hat nor an obvious sniper's nest, and beelined through the crowd, the space between his shoulder blades itching, to duck inside with the muzzle of his Winchester aimed politely at the floorboards.

The older peace officer going over some papers at a rolltop desk, like Longarm himself a federal lawman, had his own German silver badge pinned to a faded blue army shirt. He didn't act surprised to see Longarm. He nodded up at his caller and said, "If you'd be Deputy Long we've been expecting you since yesterday. If you're somebody else you sure describe like him."

Longarm said he'd been Custis Long the last time he'd gazed into his shaving mirror and asked who'd been talking about him behind his back. The Indian policeman replied, "Fort Smith wired you were coming and requested we assist you any way you might need assisting. Consider that part settled. The three strangers passing through last night said they were out to assist you as well. But I reckon they didn't feel at ease around us savages. Acted downright insulted when asked a few simple questions."

Longarm frowned thoughtfully and said, *"I'd* like to ask 'em a few simple questions, too. Did you get any names, with or without proper documentation?"

112

The Indian policeman shook his head and explained, "I didn't talk to them direct. A kid came in that same front door to tell me the three of 'em were over to the trading post, buying cut plug and asking about a white couple, male and she-male, a day or so out ahead of 'em. I got there as they were riding out. I called after 'em but they just kept going, not looking back. They hadn't done anything, here in Page, so I let it go at that. Lots of your kind ride through sort of snooty. It only occurred to us, later, they'd been talking about you and that survey gal Fort Smith told us about."

Longarm explained where Fiona was and why. The Indian agreed he'd played that hand about right. He said the three mysterious riders had a good lead if they thought they were chasing someone. He added, "If they figured they'd beat you here they could be staked out along the trail between here and our disputed border, say five miles by crow or railroad train?"

Longarm said, "You'd know better than me. Miss Coyne and me weren't planning on starting her survey from the railroad tracks. There's just no dispute about bench marks both the survey service and the K.C. Southern agree on. One of the nice things you and your own might want to do for us involves the best way to work along the main spine of the less well-mapped high country to the south."

The Indian smiled boyishly and replied, "You're right about none of those trails being on any map. We can set you straight amid the lonesome heights of the Ouachitas. We can make sure nobody west of the Arkansas line treats you mean if you'll allow a couple of dirty savages to tag along in your superior shadows."

Longarm grimaced and said, "Don't try that vanishing red man shit on me. I come here fair and square to pay a courtesy call on the local law. If you'd rather I made snide remarks 'bout shiftless reservation trash I got some good ones to pass on from some unreconstructed Lakota I know."

The Choctaw laughed and said, "Just trying to stay in practice for when I ask our Choctaw Agency for a raise. I'm serious about you and that white girl being safer with some of my boys backing your play, though. None of us are supposed to know this, lest we be called upon to do something about it, but some folk, red and white, lead mighty private lives up where the eagles nest and the winds tell ghost stories."

Longarm nodded soberly and said, "It was just such a gent, cooking mash, who told us about those three riders dogging our trail. I know how to pass a still in the pines without causing needless anxiety."

The Indian policeman rose, a tad taller than Longarm had expected him to be, insisting, "You're going to want to talk to Granny Sehoy, too. Some of our people up where the eagles nest have more important secrets than a peckerwood moonshine still and you're right about the way some less prim and proper Indians feel about lawmen of any complexion."

He hitched his gun rig to ride better and reached for the hat he'd hung on a rack near the door as he added, "No Choctaw born of mortal clay would risk the displeasure of Granny Sehoy and her quilting circle, though. So let's go ask what she thinks you and that white girl ought to do about those lost, strayed, or stolen witness trees."

Longarm didn't argue and likely asked fewer questions than some white lawmen would have as the Indian walked him out, across the road and up through some ragweed and dock to a sort of cross betwixt a bird house and a witch cottage thrown together from notched loblolly logs with the bark left on.

As they approached he did ask where the nominal male members of the tribal council might be holding that big powwow at the moment. His Choctaw informant explained, "They're not ready to get down to brass tacks, yet. Most of the old men are over in the steam lodge you're not supposed to know about, sipping Black Drink that smells more like the stuff we're not allowed to buy or sell if the truth be known. Do you really aim to wait until such time as our Tustenegee has a vision and everyone else with one gray

114

hair gets to make a speech for or against it?"

Longarm chuckled and said, "They told us you boys were civilized. The Lakota even let the *young* men argue with the poor old gents the army and B.I.A. insist on listing as chiefs."

Longarm knew better, for all the good it had ever done him or his Indian friends or foes. Men did have the final say-so among some of the horse nations as well as the truculent Nadene or Apache. But the Muskogee-speaking Choctaw, not unlike their Cherokee enemies, were matrilineal in more ways than one. A Choctaw got his personal brag-dancing and membership in one of the warrior societies, say the Red Sticks, by personal wealth or bravery, the five civilized tribes being less impressed by a poor boy with a mean streak, but at heart he'd always be a momma's boy. For the son of a Wind Clan woman would live and die Wind Clan, as respected or low-rated as his mother had been amid his kith and kin.

So it wasn't hard to figure why Muskogee speakers showed more respect than some others, red or white, to their womankind. By the time she was a grandmother a Choctaw woman expected to be treated like a queen if her sons and grandsons were worth warm spit and anyone else knew what was good for them. So Longarm had his hat off as he and the helpful Indian policeman mounted the puncheon steps of the snug little cabin.

He'd expected to meet a little old dried-up granny, without having given the matter much thought. He recovered with a poker face most Indians admired when the door popped open to reveal a right nice-looking if no longer young white lady in a calico dress and shawl of black Spanish lace. He knew she had to be Granny Sehoy when the Indian policeman she called Jacob introduced her as such.

Granny Sehoy invited them both inside, of course, and set them by her expansive fieldstone fireplace for some coffee and cake. The cake was chocolate layer, store-bought that very morn, she said. It wasn't too stale. Her coffee was a pleasanter surprise.

The Indian lawman, Jacob, started to fill the oddly attractive old lady in, in Muskogee. She told him not to be rude to their guest and added, in better English than Longarm could manage without straining, "Polly Nashoba's younger grandson, Will, dropped by already to tell me about Deputy Long and that young lady waiting for him at the Kanima spread. The Kanimas are not really Choctaw, you know, but we don't talk about that."

Longarm didn't know what she wanted to talk about. So he just went on washing down stale chocolate cake with swell coffee as the older woman settled into her own rocker, staring into the ruby coals of her small cook-fire as she continued, mostly to herself, "We Choctaw seldom intermarried with runaway darkies or trash whites. My own male ancestry includes British officers, French nobility, and a Scotch trader smart enough to play the redcoats and blue sleeves against one another. The Kanimas are all right, I suppose. But I don't see why the B.I.A. granted them and those other Muskogee allotments this far from their own talwa."

Her grandson said, soothingly, "Old Black Tom cut an Osage with a heap of kin when him and his Bessie were young, up in Creek Town, ma'am. They were fighting over Bessie, as young men will at a barn raising."

Granny Sehoy sighed and said, "You just heard me say they were all right. I'd still keep things tidier if I were in charge of the B.I.A. This southeast corner of the Nation was set aside for Choctaw and Choctaw alone. But the last time Naomi Bokchito counted, over thirty kinds of people from that many different nations have been crowded in on us by the mean old B.I.A.!"

Jacob soothed, "Ain't thirty separate nations, Granny. More like sixteen so-called tribes with some split up into nit-picky bands. If you think *we've* suffered, the B.I.A. shoved Algonquin bands into the Cherokee Strip, as if giving a big hunk of it to the Osage hadn't taught the Cherokee enough about siding with the South."

116

The Choctaw grandmother, who still looked like a middle-aged white woman to Longarm, sniffed and insisted, "It's just not fair. I was little but I still remember them promising the five civilized tribes and nobody else, red or white, would ever pester them if only they'd move out this way without another fight."

Longarm didn't think this would be the best time to bring up any treaties the Indians had broken, themselves, by smoking up federal officials and troops for that other lost cause.

Granny Sehoy bitched on, "They said everything north of the Red River and out to longitude one hundred degrees would be ours for as long as the rivers ran and the grass grew green. But they only allotted us less than one half, and that was before they started shoving Osage, Pawnee, Cheyenne, even crazy Kiowa and Comanche in with us! It's just not fair!"

Longarm assured her he knew recently whupped South Cheyenne who'd be first to agree on that. He didn't want to get into that myth about some treaty involving rivers flowing and grass growing. He'd won bar bets on that, but he still couldn't say who'd ever started the legend of George Washington in the flesh spouting anything like that to any Indian. Like most documents devised by lawyers, the few Indian treaties that hadn't been busted all to hell, by both sides, read less poetic.

But seeing she'd brought the subject up, herself, Longarm set his empty cup on the hearthstone near his boot tips and casually asked if Granny Sehoy and her quilting society were satisfied with the nearby eastern boundary of the Choctaw Strip.

She snapped, "I was until those trash whites commenced to play games about that, as well! What do you and that young lady from the survey service propose to do about that?"

He assured her, soothingly, "Set things to rights, ma'am. Miss Coyne knows more than me about finding just where she and a fresh bench mark might be on the map, so . . ."

"Women always know more than men about cutting quilts or land to measure!" the peppery old gal cut in. "Why is that poor child wasting her time with those darkies out at the Kanima spread?" she added. "Why isn't she up in the hills, where some wicked trash have cut down the witness trees? What are you menfolk going to do to them when you find out who they are?"

Longarm said, flatly; "Arrest 'em, ma'am. Destroying or moving a federal bench mark is a federal offense, punishable by a serious fine and the opportunity to make little rocks out of big ones serving at least a year at hard."

She said if it was up to her they'd hang the rascals. She sounded as if she meant it. Longarm said, "We got to catch 'em before we can do anything to 'em, ma'am. Since you seem certain they ain't Choctaw I'll not pester you about who it could be, or why. Jake, here, seems to feel Miss Coyne and me might have us some trouble running a new survey over the backbone of the Ouachitas, ma'am."

From the look the Indian gave him Longarm surmised they weren't supposed to press Granny Sehoy quite this hard. He knew she wasn't done yet when she leaned forward in her own seat to pour more coffee perilously close to his boot tips. But as he gulped it up to be more polite she turned to her grandson to ask, innocently, "Don't you mean to provide these young people an armed escort, Jacob? Honestly, there are times I could swear you boys wouldn't know right from left without a woman to set you straight!"

The Indian nodded at Longarm, saying, "That's sure a swell suggestion, Granny. I don't think I'd best leave town until this powwow breaks up, but I reckon the Hocha brothers might enjoy a few days up in the hills."

To which Granny Sehoy replied in a tone that brooked no back sass, "Buck Atoka and Roy Kenowa. Maybe you'd better deputize Malcolm Wetumka while you're at it. You just never know, and if these young people are under the protection of our clan they'd better be protected properly."

118

Chapter 12

Longarm rode back to fetch Fiona Coyne while Jacob scouted up the three Choctaw Granny Sehoy had suggested or, in point of fact, ordered.

Longarm got along better with womankind better than some men he knew. He was still convinced that did he live to be too old to give a damn he'd never understand the sweet little things. For as he rode back to town with Fiona she seemed annoyed about the extra gun hands and, hell, survey hands they'd have with them on the trail ahead.

He explained, as she pouted, "I can likely guard your pretty little ass as you set up your instruments amid the rocks and tanglewood up yonder. I sure can't hold an aiming pole for you at the same time and, correct me if I'm wrong, but won't this new survey call for you aiming that sort of tellyscope on a tripod at someone in the distance with a sort of skinny barbershop pole?"

She said that was close enough and lowered her voice, even though they were alone on the dirt wagon trace, "I was thinking about *after* a hard day's work with the silly instruments. How silly can we get after sundown, atop the covers in the moonlight, with a whole tribe of Indians gawking at us?"

He chuckled and soothed, "There'll only be three old boys tagging along and we'll have them posted farther out,'til we have a better notion who *else* might be up in those hills. Aside from the three riders who might or might not be after us with lethal intent, we've still got the person or persons unknown who seem to have, A: Destroyed the original bench marks, B: Moved them to other witness trees the original survey team never blazed, and, C: Did something as mysterious to everyone who's tried to figure out A and B, so far."

She opined it was more likely Captain Boyne had been murdered by those mysterious riders from the north than anyone where they were headed.

He frowned and demanded, "Haven't you been paying any attention, kitten? That cuss in the white planter's hat and his two wool-hatted sidekicks have already passed through these parts. They're up *ahead* of us, whatever they might have in mind."

She still seemed to think extra company might spoil their slap and tickle along the trail. He started to point out the odds could be grim, even with those three Choctaw backing him, since there was no saying how many might be backing those other three. He'd learned that when otherwise bright folk insisted on sounding dumb they generally had something they hadn't mentioned stuck in their craws.

They rode on in silence a short spell as he chose the right words. Then he demanded, "Are you sure you ain't overanxious about being a woman trying to perform chores usually reserved for men, Fiona?"

She gasped and blurted, "I can so too! I hold degrees I worked harder to earn than any smart know-it-all in pants, Custis Long!"

He laughed and said, "Hey, don't get your sweet little bowels in an uproar, Professor Coyne! I never said I knew more than you about running a survey line or quilt seam.

The Indians we'll have tagging along won't be after your job neither. You're going to have to tell the four of us how to lay your fool Gunter's chain from one new bench mark to the next, so . . ."

"Who told you about the Gunter's chain amid Captain Boyle's surveying gear?" she demanded with a wide-eyed stare.

Longarm frowned back at her and replied, "Nobody had to tell me. Neither one of you would have started an officious government survey without an officious survey chain, as designed or designated by Mr. Gunter, whoever he was, and running what, a hundred links to the rod, three hundred and twenty rods to the statute mile?"

She said, "You do know more than you let on about surveying. Are you sure they didn't send you to check up on me?"

He snorted in disbelief and replied, "No. They sent me to expose Captain Boyle as a fake surveyor with a forged degree. What's got into you, Fiona? You know your boss was alive and well when he asked for some backup in the hills ahead. What happened to him proved he'd been right about somebody not wanting him, or you, poking about for missing bench marks in the Ouachitas. I just told you, me and those Indian lawmen are only coming along to protect you. You'll be in sole command as far as the survey goes."

She demurely suggested she might not mind if he got on top, at other times. Then she demanded, defensively, "Are you going to turn me in if I make one teeny-weeny mistake, darling?"

He said he wouldn't know how to tell if she was less than ten miles off. But even as he said it he made a mental note to double-check her figures as they ran the fresh survey. He'd been telling the simple truth when he'd assured her he had no diploma in her craft. But as an army scout he'd naturally boned up on the basics of map reading or, in a pinch, map *making*. So while he could doubtless be off by a good ten yards or more, ten miles had been laying it on a mite thick.

121

They rode on a piece in awkward silence. When she asked in a little girl voice, "Penny for your thoughts?" he said something dirty enough to reassure her.

He wished someone would reassure him as he pondered the mysterious moods of womankind. It had to be she-male sensitivity about mere males teasing her about her ability to cut the mustard. He didn't think it took lots of brawn or even hairy balls to lay a straight line from here to there. He knew some men might. So the poor little thing had a right to feel anxious about getting it right with nobody disputing her skills with cross hairs, slide rule, and such.

He'd worry about her messing up more than Captain Boyle might have when he caught her messing up. He still couldn't fathom how anyone was supposed to *profit* by messing things up *deliberate!*

Chapter 13

Back in Page they were holding a pony race along the railroad service road, that year's crop of Choctaw debutantes were holding a jingle-dress dance in front of the trading post, and some old boys were beating drums in that thundersome but monotonous style most Indians preferred to black or white drumrolling. Fiona opined Choctaw women dressed more traditional but still looked whiter on average than Choctaw men. Longarm agreed, explaining, "The bone structure of young men and both sexes as they get older say more about distant ancestors. Most Muskogee speakers have more black and less white blood than they brag on. Our old South was mostly settled by English field hands who'd always aspired to be country squires. So they tried enslaving Indians as field hands, but they just run back home through the woods. So they tried importing white slaves, mostly Irish rebels or Scotch Jacobites who'd riz for Bonnie Prince Charlie. That didn't work much better. The Highland Scots in particular preferred hunting in the hills to chopping cotton and that's how come Indian war bands wound up being led by gents with names like Ross, MacIntosh, or McGillivray."

He spied old Jacob spitting and whittling out front of the police station with two younger Choctaw as he added, "Our homespun country squires back East finally settled on black slaves. They had a time getting away in serious numbers, albeit the Alabama militia had a time with a reluctant African the Indians dubbed Souanakke Tustenukke. He's in *our* history books as The Prophet or The Black Warrior. Don't ask yonder Choctaw if they might be kin to him. The Black Warrior led the Alabama Creeks, way back when."

They reined in and dismounted as Jacob and the other Choctaw stood up to shake polite. Neither of the youths the Indian policeman had recruited looked pure anything. Both were dressed like Anglo cowhands. Jacob introduced them as Roy Kenowa and Malcolm Wetumka. He said he'd found old Buck Atoka over by the sweat lodge, full of eighty proof Black Drink and in no great shape to ride, or even stand up. Longarm had to laugh at the picture. Black Drink started out as a mishmash of boiled-down holly berries, tobacco leaves, bitter-root, and what-all, meant to make one so sick he puked visions. Spiking such a brew with corn liquor had to induce visions indeed.

The two breed left were sober and said they could lead Longarm and Fiona to where things got confusing along the original survey line. The trouble had been spotted on the north slope of Rich Mountain Ridge by Choctaw coon hunters, anxious not to stray into Arkansas after anything unimportant as a coon. They'd naturally turned back, Lord-only-knew-where, when they failed to find the blazed witness trees that had ever been yonder. Malcolm said he'd been over yonder with some upset elders already. He said nobody had messed with the bench marks within sight of the railroad tracks. There was a brass marker driven into a rock outcrop, say, a mile or more south of the railroad right-of-way, after which it was anybody's guess, with no bench marks at all in some stretches while anyone with eyes to see could see brand-new ones had been blazed in oaks that had been acorns at the time of the original survey.

The two Choctaw had tethered their own ponies nearby, a tad overloaded with such bedding and possibles as a rider might feel he needed in fair weather on his own range. So nobody argued when Longarm suggested they get going, albeit both Roy and Malcolm stared at Fiona slack-jawed when she called out, *"A dol comhla, a bhalacha!"*

Longarm gently informed her your average Choctaw knew more Creole French than Gaelic. She seemed to think it dumb to give kids Celtic names if you weren't interested in such matters and demanded, "Didn't you say their old-time chiefs were Scotch-Irish?"

He said, "In olden times indeed, back East, before the proper borders of this nation were surveyed, if you take my meaning."

She did, and once they were all mounted up Malcolm Wetumka took the lead with Roy Kenowa bringing up the rear. Longarm didn't ask why. The one guide had said he knew the way. Any Choctaw curious enough about the party to pussyfoot up behind it would be dealt with best by a Muskogee speaker escorting whites through the Nation with the blessings of Granny Sehoy.

Jacob only rode a mile out of town with them before wishing them well and dropping back to keep law and order where things seemed more obviously in need of adult supervision. Malcolm led them off the already narrow trail through the pines straight at what looked to be an alder hell. Longarm, riding just ahead of Fiona, didn't call out in dismay. He knew Malcolm had mounted up sober back there and nobody tried to ride through your average alder hell unless he was blind drunk or loco en la cabeza. The western red alder only grew where its roots could get at plenty of ground water, usually, as in this case, on a north slope, fairly close to the bottom. When it *did* hit water, the thirsty alder, red or black, sprouted some more at the roots, over and over, and that was why they called the results

125

an alder hell. Trying to *cut* the springy son-of-a-bitching saplings only made them grow thicker as each stump sent up two or more buggy whips on their way to broom handles and worse. But as old Malcolm's gray gelding reached the tree line, horse and rider just kept going, the way haunts were said to walk through walls. When it was Longarm's turn he saw the nigh invisible game trail they were on followed a volcanic dike or fathom-wide seam of sooty black basalt rock the alder roots just couldn't take in. It reminded Longarm of an asphalt- and cinder-paved alley, save for being way too narrow for even an alley in more civilized parts.

The secret passage through the alder hell put them on yet another east-west pony track. When they paused an hour later for a shady trail break Longarm pointed out some busted glass just up the slope. Malcolm muttered, "You weren't supposed to notice that, White Man."

So Longarm smiled innocently and asked, "Notice what?"

The Longarm Choctaw laughed with Longarm instead of at him. Jacob had already assured them this federal lawman wasn't interested in the revenue duties on jars Indians weren't supposed to deal in to begin with.

Since they'd managed to leave Page by midafternoon there was still plenty of light left when Malcolm led them around a whetstone outcrop, reined in, and called back, "This is where they've started messing with our borders. Down that way there's no argument, all the way to the railroad and on to the north. Up the other way, over the crest of Rich Mountain, all the way down the far side, maybe as far as the upper mountain fork, somebody has been playing dirty tricks with witness trees!"

As Longarm rode closer he could see the tarnished brass spike driven flat into the fine-grained outcrop and, sure enough, inscribed with cross-lines and now barely legible numbers. Fiona dismounted nearby with a satisfied nod, saying, "I'll just make sure this bench mark's where God and the U.S. Survey Service left it last. If it is, then we'll just see who's fooling who and all and all."

Longarm knew what she needed if she really meant to start that late in the day. He said, "I'll fetch the pack pony with your sextant and such, ma'am. Malcolm, don't you agree we ought to have a lookout posted higher up, since we seem to be stopping here a good spell?"

Malcolm pointed with his chin, growling, "We've spent us some time in these hills, you know." And, sure enough, when Longarm looked about for old Roy, the fool Choctaw was already sitting a boulder like a pony, way the hell up the mountain. So Longarm just rode over to fetch the instruments Fiona needed to figure out where she was, for certain.

It took more than one. Longarm dismounted to help her set up as Malcolm tethered and tended their ponies. Together they set up and leveled her plane table, a drawing board mounted on tripod legs so's it could be tilted most any old way, albeit she said she wanted it dead level and all and all. She had a clean, lightly engraved copy of the original survey map thumbtacked to the plane table. The original bench marks were naturally already, if lightly, indicated along the Arkansas-Indian Nation line. Before confirming this particular one with her indelible pencil, Fiona sat her chronometer atop the same outcrop and broke out her brass sextant.

The afternoon sun was visible between two cedar tops to their west. As Fiona was shooting it with her sextant Malcolm joined them, smiling uncertainly. He studied the twin dials of Fiona's chronometer for a thoughtful moment, hauled out his own pocket watch, and murmured to Longarm, "No offense, but that's a piss poor mantle clock the little lady brought along. That one dial agrees with my Ingersol well enough. But the other's over six hours off!"

Longarm softly explained, "That's what time it is in Greenwich, near London Town. Miss Fiona's checking the local time by the sun, knowing how high it's supposed to be at a given time of day, this time of the year at this latitude an' all."

The Choctaw said, "Oh. Wouldn't it be way easier to just get a clock that stayed accurate?"

Longarm laughed and said, "Those two dials are accurate as clockwork can be made. They're called chronometers or time measurers because they measure time to the split second. The dial set at Greenwich time is left that way no matter where Miss Fiona roams. She keeps resetting the second dial to keep time with the rotating of this earth wherever she may be. The difference betwixt the two dials tells her how far east or west she might be of zero longitude or a line drawn pole to pole through Greenwich, England, see?"

The Choctaw must have. He brightened and said, "Well, I never. So that's how you tell how far east or west you may be? What about north and south, do you want to find yourself on that bitty map?"

Fiona had been listening. As she turned their way to reset her chronometer she dimpled at Malcolm and explained, "To check how far off your compass might be, and it's always a few degrees off, you wait until dark and shoot the North Star. It's easier than shooting the sun at any time but high noon and all and all. The North Star never strays from its place in the night sky. But it seems to be higher or lower as one moves north and south around the bulge of the earth, so . . ."

"I swan!" grinned Malcolm, "There ain't half as much to this survey stuff as I feared."

Longarm and Fiona exchanged glances. She smiled softly and said, "Fortunately nobody cares about north or south right now. Just let me consult my tables and make an educated guess how far east or west we may be of where this bench mark was driven to begin with."

She produced a pocket almanac, checked her figures thrice, then made a triumphant little X on her pinned-down map, saying, *"Is seo math!* If anyone's moved this bench mark imbedded in bedrock they haven't moved it far enough to measure. I don't see any other suitable outcrops around here, do you, boys?"

Longarm said, "Not with holes driven into 'em. They said the old bench marks downslope to the north are still in place, too, remember?"

Fiona set her sextant aside and swung the alidade, or surveyor's transit built into one edge of her plane table, around to aim it up the slope toward their distant Choctaw lookout, muttering half to herself, "There's supposed to be a tree, a tall one, rising between us and that rock Roy's perched on."

The nearby Choctaw told her, "It ain't, ma'am. Not even a stump left, now. But see that big popple, over to the left of Roy? That's been blazed and marked with Roman numbers fairly neat."

Fiona adjusted her cross hairs on the tree he'd indicated, even as she protested, "We don't use Roman numerals and even if we did who'd ever use a short-lived weed tree and, even if they did, that poplar's a good four hundred yards inside Arkansas!"

Longarm sighed and said, "I made it a tough rifle shot, too. We'd best set about making camp, Malcolm. The day's about shot and we figure to be here some time, now."

Chapter 14

They supped before sundown with the Choctaw boys changing places as Fiona dished out warm beans, hot coffee, and
some cold hush puppies their Choctaw guides had brought
along. Both liked sugar and canned cow in their Arbuckle.
Roy said he'd heard some Osage still put white flour and
even salt in their coffee, which only served to show the
infernal Osage were Sioux at heart, for all their cotton shirts
and fancy roping.

Longarm wasn't sure he approved or disapproved of
the speed with which the Indian Nation was turning into
Oklahoma Territory, as they now called those parts further
west thrown open to white homesteaders. He suspected that
ere long it would be tough to tell where one left off and
the other began, as the five civilized tribes got more so and
the white sodbusters and stockmen got wilder, in country
Mother Nature had never designed with sissies in mind.

After supper, there still being plenty of gloaming left,
Longarm walked Fiona up to that weed tree someone had
blazed so odd. They left her instruments in camp, against

that whetstone outcrop. There was no argument about it being way out of line. Up close, in fair light, Longarm estimated and Fiona agreed the poor poplar, no more than fifteen years of age, had been blazed mayhaps the summer before last, judging by how its exposed sapwood had weathered from milk white to dirty gray. Fiona said the Roman numerals incised in the flat expanse of wood meant nothing at all, even to a Roman. As soon as she'd pointed it out, Longarm agreed there was no such Roman number as VIXMIII. He frowned and said, "That's just pointless, unless it's supposed to be a problem for Roman schoolkids to solve."

Fiona tried, "Six minus ten plus one thousand and three, dear?"

He got out his notebook to write that down, in both breeds of numerals, muttering, "It works better as some sort of code than as sheer numerical nonsense. On the other hand, what sense was there in destroying the original witness tree and . . . Let's drift over to where this poplar should have been standing, as an oak."

They moved west along the slope, the thick forest duff soft underfoot. About where he'd have been had he been born an oak tree fit for bench-marking, he spotted what might have been the outlines of a stump but, on closer inspection, it was only the ring-shaped remains of a long-gone sycamore or gum, no more suitable for the survey service than that mysterious popular. So they scouted about some more, scuffing the duff to bare dirt with their boot tips, in vain.

Longarm swore softly and said, "Let's say they cut her down to her roots and then dug up the roots. There still ought to be some sign and I'll be switched if I can read any. How do you like the notion the original witness tree was that ancient sycamore?"

She said, "I don't. That's one of the reasons Captain Boyle asked for me when he saw I knew one tree from another. The original survey team had orders to blaze solid rock wherever possible and solid oak where not. As you can see from right here, these hills are wooded with mostly cedar, hickory, locust, and oak, if you're talking about real trees. Osage orangewood lasts but the trees are pretty modest. This other trash, alder, poplar, sycamore, and all and all would be a waste of time and effort, dear."

He thought, kicked at the only sign a tree had ever sprouted within yards, and said, "I've seen sycamores forty or fifty years old."

She shrugged and said, "They last longer than that in a churchyard or public square. But not on the north slope of a windswept mountain. They'd have never blazed any silly sycamore and, *a mo mala, seo!*"

He moved over to where she'd dropped to one denim-clad knee to poke at some bitty mushrooms he knew you didn't want to eat. He said, "They ain't poison but they're bitter as bile if you're planning on picking 'em, kitten."

She said, "I'm not. Look how they're growing, in a dear little ring more than a yard across."

He pursed his lips and decided, "Maybe. I know mushrooms like to grow over oak tree roots. I'd still feel better if I saw an oak tree within a quarter mile."

She rose, saying it hardly mattered, now that they'd have to find another solid surface to leave a fresh bench mark. They agreed the light was getting tricky for that and headed back down the slope to where they'd left their ponies and at least one Choctaw.

Longarm was mildly annoyed to see both Malcolm and Roy near the cook-fire, until he noticed they were jawing with a big, bulky white boy wearing bib overalls, a wool hat, and a ten-gauge shotgun.

As the white couple joined them Malcolm said, "There you go, Tiny. I told you me and Roy was scouting for the Great White Father. These folks are running a new survey for him and as anyone can plainly see they're white as you and Mr. Beelzebub."

"That's Beverwick, you half-witted half-breed!" The giant dubbed Tiny rumbled. "Whether these folk are white or just

132

white-looking like half you rascals don't cut no ice. Ain't it a fact that you're trespassing on Arkansas and ain't it a fact your tribe's been holding a war dance just the other side of the line when everybody knows they're supposed to meet Tuskahoma with their Indian agent's permit and . . ."

"I'd be U.S. Federal Deputy Custis Long," Longarm cut in, adding, "This here's Miss Fiona Coyne of the U.S. Survey Service and we're here to find out who might be trespassing where, precise. According to a brass marker you can't see from here in this light, the five of us are a tad east of the Arkansas state line, as you suggest."

Tiny said, "I ain't suggesting nothing. I'm saying it plain."

Longarm said, "I ain't finished saying my say. According to a witness tree you can't see from here, either, you and that scatter gun have strayed a good three or four hundred yards inside the Indian Nation."

The large, lardy youth protested, "Hold on, I reckon I know east from west and from time immortal that whetstone outcrop, ahint you, has marked the easternmost limits of the Nation. It says so in writing on a brass plug druv in the rock!"

Longarm nodded but insisted, "Miss Coyne's official survey map says the line runs almost due north from a vanished oak we just paid a call on, up the slope a ways. So before anyone starts a border war we'd best make sure just where said border might be."

Tiny scowled and said, "I know the witness tree you're talking about. I don't hunt or gather a lawsome inch west of it."

Longarm soothed, "I'm sure you don't, intentional. But is it safe to say you've been staying east of a beeline running from say yonder outcrop to that poplar tree with the Roman numbers blazed on it?"

Tiny nodded and said, "Sure I have. The line runs north and south from bench mark to bench mark, like you said. It ain't hard to stay east or west of a north-south line, if you've a mind to."

Longarm turned to Fiona, muttering, "Shall I, or would you rather?"

Fiona smiled up at the troubled youth to explain, "The true line runs a tad to the west of due south, from that outcrop. That poplar, aside from being far too young and bearing far too new a blaze, is way to the east of where the original witness tree must have stood. I can see how someone just running the ridges without even a magnetic compass could assume an imaginary line from here to there was close enough."

She pointed at her tripod, just visible, now, against the whetstone outcrop as she soothed, "I could let you see for yourself if it was still daylight. But I fear you'd never be able to make out the cross hairs in this light."

Longarm saw she was confusing the not-too-bright Tiny more than she was reassuring him. So he said, "You and your friends and neighbors are free to watch as we survey things right around here. We could use some help, holding aiming poles, dragging chains, and such. Most of all I'd like to jaw with folk who know these hills whilst Miss Coyne and the boys get things pinned neater. You know other witness trees, on up the line from that one we've been jawing about?"

Tiny said, "Sure I do. That's how you tell when you're straying too close to the Indian Nation. I never hunt in the Nation for Mr. Beverwick. He's ordered us direct not to."

"What are you after with that scatter gun and no dogs? Deer?" asked Longarm conversationally.

Tiny looked, if possible, more confused. Malcolm laughed and said, "Bees. Wild honeybees for his boss, old Mr. Beelzebub."

Tiny almost wailed, "That's *Beverwick,* you dumb Choctaw!"

But Malcolm insisted, "Ain't honeybees the white man's flies and don't it say in the Good Book that Beelzebub was the lord of the flies?"

Longarm saw the teasing was upsetting the big, dumb kid more than Malcolm likely intended. He nudged the Choctaw to silence him as he told the white youth, soothingly, "He was only funning. I think I've tasted some of Mr. Beverwick's honey. He sells some to the trading post in Page, right?"

Tiny nodded and said, "Sells *all* of it, yonder. The white settlers around the next stop, east, raise such bees themselves, as they have need for."

Fiona said she'd had some of that honey, too, and thought it was delicious. Tiny said he was glad and that now he had to get on down the mountain to put Mr. Beverwick to bed.

Longarm didn't question him on that. As he'd hoped, the giant was barely out of sight through the trees before Malcolm explained, "The poor old cuss Tiny works for gets more helpless by the day. He had him one of them brain strokes a spell back. Been rocking-chair-bound for a couple of years."

Roy Kenowa corrected, "He's had more than *one* such seizure. Be dead for certain had not Granny Sehoy sent over the right medicine bark to mix with the honey and vinegar he was already dosing with. Willow bark is good for brain strokes. You'd think more white sawbones would know that."

Fiona said she was starting to feel chilled. They all moved closer to the fire and Malcolm threw some cedar on for sudden flaring as he said, "Be that as it may, the old beekeeper's lucky to have Tiny working for him and vice versa. Tiny would have a time getting hired as a stable hand. They say the old man still has to tend his bees and extract the honey neat. Tiny's too dumb to notice he's getting stung but would anyone want to buy a jar of honey he'd messed up with bits of comb-wax, baby bees, and worse?"

"What's that part about him *hunting* bees?" asked Longarm.

Malcolm explained, "Wild ones, hiving. You'd have to ask old Mr. Beelzebub why bees do that, but every now and again a whole swarm of wild bees get to hanging on some tree branch, like a big buzzing beard. Tiny runs down the mountain to fetch Mr. Beelzebub whenever he hunts down such a swarm. The crippled-up old man's a caution when it comes to handling the little stingsome buzzers. I don't know how he does it but he can get the whole swarm into a pasteboard box or even his hat without getting stung. Then Tiny totes him back home and they get them another hive going in his bee yard by the railroad tracks. Ain't that a bitch?"

"Bee gums!" Longarm muttered, half to himself. Fiona casually took him by one arm, yawned elaborately, and said, "I'm awfully cold and it's been a long day. But, all right, what's a bee gum?"

He said, "Usually a sour gum tree grown old and hollow in these parts. Sycamores make good bee trees, too."

Both Choctaw boys laughed. Malcolm said, "I helped my Uncle Dan and some of the other men raid a bee gum when I was little. Like to got my fool self stung to death. But that wild honey was sure good, once we got it out of that old bee gum!"

Longarm said, "I'll bet it was, and you didn't leave much of the tree *standing,* did you?"

It was Fiona's turn to catch on. But she protested, "Nobody would be dumb enough to blaze a sycamore or pepperidge. That's what we call your sour gum in polite society. You're right about them both being notorious for heart rot and . . ."

"Worth a visit to the old beekeeper," Longarm cut in. "It's a short ride down by the tracks from here. It'll keep getting longer as you survey south. Right now you've got the boys, here, to keep you safe the short while I'll be gone."

She protested it was late and that she wanted to go to bed. He told her to go ahead. She still followed him over to the pony line and that gave him the chance to privately assure her, as he saddled that paint, "I'll be back way this side of midnight and guess where I mean to lay my own sleepy head?"

She sighed and said, "If you're not back soon I may just start without you and, honestly, Custis, how many trees blazed along one survey line could wind up hollow and infested by bees in less than half a century?"

He glanced about, saw they were alone, save for the ponies, and kissed her good before he explained, "I know it's a wild possibility. You'd be surprised how wild possibles can get in my line of work and I'm paid to check everything possible off my list. I don't think an old crippled beekeeper named after Satan has been converting witness trees to beehives, either. But I'd best make sure."

Chapter 15

Finding the Beverwick homestead near the railroad right-of-way was easy. Even if it hadn't been right about where he'd expected it, Longarm would have spotted the window lights from farther off than he was when he rode out of the trees onto the service road south of the tracks. The cheerfully bright windows were just a furlong east. A dog started yapping long before he got there. As he reined in out front, Tiny reappeared in the doorway, still packing that ten-gauge, to call out, "We know you're there, dad blast your Choctaw hides!"

Longarm called out, "I come in peace from the Great White Father, Tiny. It's me, Long. Wanted a word in private with your boss."

Tiny stepped out on the porch, grumbling, "Mr. Beverwick's already turnt in. He ain't been well, you know."

Longarm dismounted anyway, insisting, "It's not much after sundown and this could be important, Tiny."

The husky youth went right on barring the door with his considerable bulk and shotgun, growling, "I just got him tucked away for the night. It wasn't easy. The poor old gent's been sick as a dog for a coon's age and it's hard to fall asleep after all you've been doing all day wouldn't tire a babe-in-arms. I have to give him opium pills with his corn liquor afore he'll even close his eyes and I'll fight you if you try to wake him up again after all I've done, hear?"

Longarm sighed and said, "I don't want to fight you, Tiny. Let's try it another way. You say you hunt wild bees for your crippled-up employer. Might that include wild bees hived rich in hollow trees?"

Tiny said, "Sometimes you stumble over a bee gum or heart-rotted sycamore. Mr. Beverwick says never to tell on the bees when I do. Wild honey raided outten a tree ain't as fine as what we raise out back to sell clean and clear in mason jars and, besides, bees don't swarm as often if they're raided."

Longarm thought back to some otherwise pointless reading in a lawyer's office before he said, "Let me see if I've got this right. Your boss would rather be kind to wild bees and tame the extra swarms from such hollow trees as you know of?"

Tiny said that was about the size of it and added he'd found way more swarms just swarming than around any known bee gum. He explained that once a queen bee was driven from the main swarm with her own bunch they might fly for miles before they settled down somewhere to rest and, if they were really lucky, wind up in one of the old beekeeper's patent hives, out back. Tiny added, "Mr. Beverwick makes me hammer new hives together tight from new lumber. I tried to clean out some supers that had suffered the pest and use 'em again. He said he'd fire me if I ever did that again. He said the bee pest was spread by bitty bugs you couldn't see and . . ."

"We've agreed your boss is fond of bees," Longarm cut in, tempted to just move the well-meaning moron out of his way and bull on in for more sensible words with the old beekeeper. But on reflection he decided an angry or

139

bewildered old man, aroused from opium dreams, might not make a lick more sense. So he settled for saying, "All right. You know where we're camped. It'll likely take us the better part of tomorrow getting any distance up the ridge, peering through transits at aiming poles, dragging chains, and so on. In the morning, when your boss wakes up, I want you to ask him if he or anyone else ever noticed a bee gum along that old survey line. I know it sounds silly, but if someone cut a witness tree down on public land for private reasons they just might try to cover up by marking another, nearby, as best they knew how, see?"

Tiny laughed—it hurt to have someone that stupid laughing at one—and said, "I'll ask, but I know what he'll say. No matter who marked what, all them witness trees I've ever seen have been hardwood, such as oak or other nut trees. Never gum. Pine don't make good bee trees, neither."

Longarm had to agree, even if it was annoying to be lectured on botany by a lout who likely couldn't spell T.R.E.E. That reminded him of someone prettier with a degree in botany. So he settled for, "Well, someone's been cutting down trees and blazing others for some damned reason. It is public land and fifty- or sixty-year-old specimens of the species you mentioned would be worth something, this close to a rail line. Meanwhile it's been nice talking to you, Tiny."

Tiny turned around to step back inside and slam the door in Longarm's face. Longarm muttered, "Up your own, you poor half-wit," and stepped off the porch to mount up so he could go get laid.

Next morning after breakfast and considerable dithering with cross hairs it was Longarm, in the end, who saw a simple solution to what struck him as a simple problem. Unlike Fiona and the earlier survey team that had proceeded her by many a long year, Longarm wasn't set in his surveying ways by book-learning. After Fiona had fumed and fussed with her plane table a spell he asked her for a look-see through her alidade. She'd already said it was lined up with the slightly off north-south line on her fool map. As he peered through the sort of half-ass telescope she was saying, "You can see there's simply not a suitable tree, let alone an outcrop, this side of that distant slab of sedimentary rock."

He said, "Yep, you got this thing sighted just about dead center on that hogback atop that next ridge. So what's the matter with using *that?* Don't you reckon we could drive one of them brass stakes into slate if we put our backs into it?"

She said, "That's not the point, Custis. The bench mark indicated on this map of the original survey falls at least a chain and a half short of that rock slab, see?"

To which he could only reply, "Nope. We've been upslope to where they blazed that old bench mark and anyone can see there's nothing there worth marking, now. You ain't allowed to just drive a brass stake into the top soil and hope for the best, are you?"

She laughed incredulously and said, "We have enough trouble getting kids or rooting hogs to leave out *solidly* placed ones alone. My point exactly is that we need something solid, within inches if not right on the line, to . . ."

"Let's mark that rock-solid hogback, then," he insisted.

She said, "Damn it, Custis, it's nowhere near the original bench mark. Haven't you been paying any attention?"

He said, "Yep. You and the late Captain Boyle were sent down here to resurvey that fool line and make sure any bench marks left along it were set proper."

She started to repeat her basic mistake. He said, "I ain't finished. We can't expect anyone to use a witness tree that ain't there to keep from hunting bees in the Indian Nation. Another bench mark, inscribed on brass in solid rock, ought to convince most anyone. I know that hogback's a tad farther south than the missing witness tree could have been. It's still on the same fool *line,* ain't it?"

She started to offer the obvious objection, then proved how much common sense she had, after all, by clapping

141

her hands and saying, "Of course! We only have to take a new linear measurement from here to there and map it as a brand-new but still accurate bench mark!"

So that was what they did. The Choctaw boys were a great help with the sixty-six-foot Gunter, a literal steel chain with a hundred links.

Longarm didn't see how he and Fiona could have managed alone. He hadn't forgotten those three mysterious riders. He insisted at least one male member of the party keep watch at all times whilst the others manhandled the more complicated than heavy gear through the woods.

Some of it included square brass marker stakes like the old one down the slope in that whetstone outcrop. They used a maul and star drill to drive a pilot hole for another through slate that rang like boilerplate as they took turns hammering. Then at last the second of likely many bench marks was in place and things got even more tedious. For, as Fiona kept complaining, shifting the second bench mark threw things off so they had to measure every infernal inch to some damned something solid on that old survey map.

Knowing how far the new mark was from the old, they had to stake their way on, the way Fiona's cross hairs said to, dragging the heavy Gunter on and on, counting off eighty chain lengths to the mile as Fiona fussed about missing bench marks.

They agreed the one that should have been about a quarter mile south of that slate hogback had been either a monstrous buckeye or a more modest oak. Either stump would do, allowing for what Fiona called inevitable deviation. One of the Choctaw found a fair-sized locust blazed and incised with more of those Roman numerals, a good fifty yards inside the Indian Nation, according to Fiona.

Malcolm demanded, "How come? There's nobody using this neck of the woods for anything on either side of the line? Why would anyone want to cheat Arkansas by a rifle shot down that way and then take away a pretty good strip of Indian land, here?"

142

Longarm decided, "That locust was the nearest big tree handy. None of these second growth saplings closer to this swamping buckeye stump looks half as convincing."

He braced a boot up on the flat, cleanly sawed stump to proclaim, "I vote we drive another official marker into this still solid heartwood and X the same spot on your map, ma'am."

Fiona stared down dubiously, deciding, "Well, this nut tree must have already been tall timber when that first crew came through here years ago. But what about that oak stump, Custis?"

He shook his head and said, "Too small. I know you said they tell you survey folk to use oak if you can get it. If that blackjack was still a sapling they'd have used this way more impressive buckeye. It's a kissing cousin to chestnut and chestnut lasts even longer than oak when you study on it. I'm betting they studied on it, way back when, and chose this big old buckeye as their witness tree."

He reached for a smoke as he added, wearily, "Don't nobody ask me why someone else cut it down and marked another in its place. As fast as locust grows, that one wasn't on this mountain way back when."

Fiona nodded and said, "Let's do it, then. Where did I last see that saddlebag with the brass markers?"

Roy Kenowa picked it up from the forest duff near one end of the sprawled-out Gunter and brought it to them, saying, "I'd best go back and move the ponies again, seeing we're fixing to move on."

Longarm glanced at such sky as he could make out through the tree branches above. He said, "Leave 'em be for now, Roy. It's going on noon. We'll just mark this stump and you and Malcolm can start us all some coffee on that last fire, down the other side of that hogback."

The young Choctaw started to object, looked around as if to get his bearings, and decided, "You're right. We ain't moved more than a mile and a half all morning and a short stroll beats moving a whole camp."

He started down through the trees. Malcolm asked if they didn't want him to help up this way. Longarm told him to run along and that he and Miss Fiona would join them down the mountain shortly.

The Choctaw tried not to grin too knowingly as he turned away.

As Longarm knelt to take out a brass marker and get to work Fiona almost sobbed, "You may as well have come right out and said you meant to fuck me atop this stump at high noon, you brute!"

Longarm grinned and told her, "Don't tempt me. I had something sneakier in mind. I know this job means a heap to you and secrets keep best betwixt two than four."

She gasped, "Then you've noticed the way they've been talking behind our backs, in Choctaw?"

He said, "They ain't been talking behind our backs. They've been joshing in their own dialect, likely dirty, right in front of us. I doubt either boy means anyone any harm, kitten. It's just that we're going to have to cut some corners if we're ever to get done with this fool survey. What Roy just said about taking all morning to measure less than two country miles was all too true, and to be honest with you I'm more interested in who's been tinkering with this border line, and why, than just how tight you might want to draw it on yonder map."

She glanced over at her plane table, asking what he had in mind. So he said, "Let's run things more by guess and by God, estimating the distance betwixt bench marks instead of counting off the distance link by link."

She protested, "Custis, an innacurate survey is worse than no survey at all!"

He soothed, "I never said we ought to mark anywheres but along the damned *line*. I'm saying the distance betwixt one marker and another ain't important, next to keeping the local whites and Indians out of each other's hair. I mean, if you put up gateposts everyone can see, does it matter just how near or far the damn posts might be from one another?"

She said it mattered to her superiors. He said, "All right, try her this way. Say we survey my way, just making certain we have the *line* right. Then say we report it as no more than that and let them double-check the distances bewixt your new markers later, once things are calmer?"

She said she'd have to think about that. So he pounded the brass marker into the old buckeye stump, flush with the still-solid heartwood. By the time he'd finished she said, "I suppose if you backed my rough estimate, saying you'd deputized me or something . . ."

He said, "There you go, kitten. Do we just draw another bead with your cross hairs from here and guess how far the next bench mark would have been, unless we find another stump solid as this one, of course, we can make it down to where the line's still undisputed and back in no more than say two days and nights in this tanglewood."

She sighed and said she might have known he'd have tired of her already. He told her he wasn't tired of her. He was only tired of investigating such a tedious mystery without even an educated guess as to who was doing what, and why.

She didn't seem convinced, even when he assured her he'd have been at her already if she hadn't had those manly jeans on. So he figured the least he could do was lead her into some loblolly and haul down those manly jeans to treat her manly before lunch.

Chapter 16

Fiona was willing, once he'd joined her in his bedroll, spread near that outcrop just outside the ruby glow of the night fire. Roy Kenowa was out a ways on picket. Malcolm lay slugabed or jacking off on the other side of camp. After Longarm and Fiona had managed a protracted, and hence delightful, quiet orgasm she complained the boys had been talking about them in Choctaw, earlier.

He kissed her soothingly, leaving it in her for now, as he asked how she knew what the boys might or might not have been discussing in their own Indian dialect.

Fiona adjusted her legs around his waist more casually as she replied, *"A mo mala* and how did you think I learned so much of the Gaelic as a girl growing up on this side of the pond? My parents always switched to the Gaelic when they didn't want us kids to know what they were talking about and all and all. It's the dirty words and phrases the older kids taught us in the schoolyard and once you develop a great interest in what your darling mother might be after saying in the dark, the rest falls into place."

He laughed and moved in her experimentally, asking how one might describe what he was doing to her in the Gaelic.

She started moving in time with his thrusts, confiding, "Jig a jig is close as it gets to fuck and in point of fact it can signify dancing as well. It's almost impossible to translate dirty English words and phrases into the Gaelic. It has no words that are dirty as they stand, alone, like fuck, shit, or piss. You have to use a little imagination to insult someone in the Gaelic."

He said, "Reminds me of Spanish or, come to study on it, most Indian dialects I know well enough to cuss in. You can call a Mex *hijo de perra* but it somehow loses the bite of son of a bitch. To really talk mean in Spanish you have to say something about pissing on the grave of someone's father, if anyone knew who his father really was."

Fiona murmured, "Ooh, that feels just right and the way you'd let someone know how you felt about them in Gaelic would call for the same strategy. The Gaelic for bastard is the same as English, or French, without, as you say, the bite. If you really wanted to start a fight you might sweetly suggest a man go home to comfort his dear old mother, who's had no sex since he and the pig ran away."

Longarm finished coming in her before he groaned, "We don't have that problem, do we?"

She moaned, "Oh, Jesus, Mary, and Joseph, me too, and it feels better every time you do it to me! But what about those Indians? I tell you I'm sure they know about us, darling!"

He kissed her again and murmured, "I'd be worried about 'em if I thought they had us down as brother and sister. Of course they know. They knew we'd been on the trail, alone, when Jacob recruited 'em to guide us. Didn't you just say you used to listen to your mother and father saying dirty things in the dark?"

She confided, "I did, and there were times at the breakfast table I couldn't meet their eyes. I was sure they knew I knew they'd been dirty and . . ."

"They weren't being dirty, they'd been fucking," he cut in, with a suggestive thrust as well. "They were a healthy couple in bed together, doing what comes natural, not dirty. Those Choctaw boys are more assimilated than say Paiute or Comanche, but they've still grown up sort of country, next to you, I suspect. Most members of the five civilized tribes have been Christian for some time, but they're less inspired than some in these parts to roll in the aisles and speak in tongues about dirty little secrets or rattlesnakes. I'm sure Malcolm and Roy know why men and women are built so different. They have to know Granny Sehoy never produced all those grandchildren without any masculine help. Yet they still respect her as if she was some sort of Choctaw saint."

Fiona hugged him to her tighter, saying, "I'm not an old Indian lady. What if they *don't* respect me? What if they want to do *this* to me and all and all?"

He shrugged his bare shoulder and replied, "They likely do, if they have any imagination at all. But they won't try, if they know what's good for 'em and, Jesus H. Christ, Fiona, don't we have enough other things to worry about?"

Chapter 17

Longarm's rougher way resulted in way faster progress through the mighty rough country. It was still way slower than even a careful deer stalk on foot, since Fiona insisted they walk the invisible line as carefully as if it had been a tight wire over Niagara and Longarm agreed they ought to get *that* part right, at least.

So one or the other Choctaw had to scamper ahead through the trees to where Fiona was just able to keep him and a ten-foot aiming pole in her eyepiece. Then she'd wave him left or right to where he was holding it smack betwixt Arkansas and the Indian Nation. After that, all they had to do was drive a smaller disposable stake in the forest duff, tote her gear that far, set it up some more, and start all over. She felt way better a day further along, on the far side of Rich Mountain Ridge, when they came upon a still-standing witness tree blazed by the original survey team. It was a gnarly old oak with its bark grown almost all the way over the original bench mark, a numbered copper nail driven to bull's-eye old cross lines weathered almost invisible against the time-blackened but still sound wood.

When Fiona checked her newer map against the old bench mark she announced they were smack on the line and about as far south of that last new bench mark she'd left in yet another buckeye stump as she'd hoped.

Knowing where they were, even if it was in a second growth tangle all cut up by headwater creeks of the eventually westward flowing Kiamachi, they found their way to where the next witness tree stood on Fiona's map. None of them were too surprised to find nothing there but a few scattered stumps amid mostly hickory saplings, with a fair-sized sycamore freshly blazed and marked with those apparently pointless Roman numerals a good pistol shot deep in the Indian Nation.

Fiona agreed the stump Longarm picked was in about the right place and would have been an impressive tree half a century before. But again it looked to be a buckeye, not an oak.

Longarm nodded and said, "I've been studying on that. Most of the oak at this altitude seems to be blackjack of less than impressive dimensions. Whether the old-timers laying this border out for Andrew Jackson knew one tree from another or not, they'd have been way more impressed by big old buckeyes, and ain't buckeye wood used to make coffins as well as less likely to be abused furniture?"

She regarded the stump he'd hooked an instep on with a thoughtful frown as she leafed through botany texts in her memory a spell before deciding, "When freshly sawn, buckeye lumber resembles white pine, save for being even softer, weaker, and, as you just pointed out, fairly resistant to decay, wet or dry."

He nodded and said, "There you go. I vote we make this stump official. Now if only I could figure out who cut it down, and why they marked that fool sycamore, yonder."

Fiona said, "That sycamore's apt to rot away before this stump, now that its bark's been blazed so deep in its sapwood."

Longarm muttered he'd just said that and called Roy over to hand him a brass spike to pound into the stump. As Roy held it for him Longarm studied the way the witness tree had been felled with a saw. A two-man whipsaw, from the thickness of the stump and its neat flat top. He said, "Roy, you'd know better than me about the lumber industry in your Nation. Don't this watershed lead eventual to the Kiamachi and don't the Kiamachi lead in turn to your main Choctaw settlements around the Tuskahoma Agency?"

The young Choctaw said, "By way of Pine Valley, Albion, and Kiamachi. We like to think of our capitol as a talwa rather than an agency. But in any case we're talking forty or fifty miles if you're talking about rafting timber that far."

"I am," said Longarm. "A tree the size of this missing witness tree adds up to a heap of felled timber and as you can see, there's nothing bigger than wrist-thick windfall all around."

Roy shook his head and said, "Nobody's been rafting witness trees or any other kind of trees down the Kiamachi to more settled country. To begin with nobody would have to. There's plenty of timber way closer. After that the Kiamachi is a sometimes stream. Deep and dangerous after thunder on the mountain and barely enough water for crawdads during a dry spell."

Fiona, who'd been listening, asked if it wasn't more likely the mysteriously missing trees had been felled and hauled away by whites from east of the line. Longarm agreed the Indians shouldn't have lodged the original complaint if *all* of them had been in on it, but added, "I'd go with a casual logging of government land if I could figure how to get such big logs out of here without reducing 'em to cordwood. There's no wagon trace or even a skid row, this side of the ridge. The railroad's on the far side of said ridge. So even if somebody had a secret deal with say an ambitious train crew, why would they go to that much trouble and, if they did want to haul heavy full-grown timber clean over a mountain ridge, why would they pick on witness trees to begin with?"

He'd said that while hammering the square spike flush. As they straightened up, Roy Kenowa suggested, "Maybe the witness trees were the last big old trees left?"

Fiona laughed incredulously and waved expansively at the tall timber all around. But Longarm nodded thoughtfully and said, "From the mouths of babes and I meant that friendly, Roy. These timbered hills we see today ain't the same as they would have been at the time of Old Hickory and the Trail of Tears. A mess of whites have moved out this way as well since then, whether they like to settle within sight of Indian nations or not."

Fiona asked why he was offering them a history lesson on history they already knew. He said, "This ain't the historic period of the original survey. Most of what's growing along the line right now is second, mayhaps third growth after the original virgin forest was culled for prime logs or, right along the line, preserved to be witness trees. So don't laugh at old Roy just yet. Some slickers cruising for timber betwixt then and now might well have simply *stole* the best timber still standing, see?"

Fiona shook her head and said, "We're arguing in circles, Custis. I thought you and Roy just agreed a timber operation this far from civilization or even a decent road wouldn't be practical."

Longarm sighed and said, "When you're right you're right. I'm just going to have to catch 'em and ask 'em. Roy, why don't you move out to find Malcolm? I'd say it was your turn to watch out for those three white riders who preceded us to these parts."

Roy said he doubted that, seeing they hadn't cut the sign of one strange pony, let alone three. But he still trotted off through the trees before Longarm could tell him you weren't supposed to cut sign if the other side knew what they were doing. Being an Indian, Roy had likely been told that already.

By the time Malcolm drifted in to join them, Fiona had set up again with her tripod straddling the old buckeye stump.

Longarm hadn't sent Roy out on picket to overwork him. The boys liked to change chores the same as anyone else. Malcolm had just commenced to find the birdsong boring out in the woods when he got to work with the aiming pole some more. Fiona couldn't send either of them ahead as far, in this neck of the woods. The second growth got enough rain and way more sun on these mostly southward-facing slopes. So there were way more leaves as well as more bugs and erosion gullies had no respect at all for the string-straight line betwixt red and white territory.

Helping Fiona across a deep one with her gear, he saw what Roy meant about thunder on the mountain. There wasn't any, at the moment, so the twisty stream bed lay dry and dusty as well as deep. He made a mental note to move their camp again well this side of sundown, lest they bust a pony leg or more in such treacherous going.

They'd worked their way a mile or so on down when Fiona spied an impressive stump rising like a butte from among a tangle of ferns but, when she said, "That looks like another ancient buckeye," Longarm said, "It does, but it ain't in the right place for a witness tree."

She didn't believe him until she'd set up her fool plane table and sited back up the line to their last bench mark. Once she had she marveled, "You're right. This one's way east of the line as well as at least a chain too short of where it's supposed to be. But how did you do that, Custis?"

He shrugged and modestly replied, "Told you I've done some army scouting. I don't know enough about mapping to call myself a pro, like you. But I've been keeping count of my own pacing and landmarks the far side of your point of aim as we've been wandering through the trees."

Malcolm, who'd wandered even farther with his aiming staff, called up at them, "There's another tree blazed Roman style, down here."

Fiona didn't have to draw a bead on the one he'd leaned his pole against to determine it was way out of line. As they strode down to join the Choctaw they spotted not one but three good-sized buckeye stumps amid the ferns. Longarm said he was sure she'd be able to figure out which one had been the witness tree. She scowled at all three as she demanded, "Why buckeyes, whether they were blazed by us or not?"

Malcolm asked what she meant. Longarm explained, "They left a witness tree alone when it was an oak. Some such missing trees could have been most anything. You can't say when a tree's been gone since before the war. But every one we've relocated for certain seems to have been a buckeye and, now that I study on it, have either of you seen buckeye growing anywheres around here, *on* the line or *off* it?"

Neither of them had. Fiona said, "That's downright spooky, Custis. I just agreed buckeye lumber's all right for knocking together household furniture or coffins. But it's not nearly as valuable as oak, cedar, or even hickory and there's plenty of that still standing, some large enough to log and . . ."

"They ain't been logging these slopes, recent," Longarm cut in. Pointing at her plane table, he continued, "That survey map don't show it but I perused some plain old maps on my way here and so I can tell you we're discussing logging operations in the middle of nowheres much. We're a good ten miles or more from the nearest Indian settlement at Pine Valley, which has no railroad connections. Right, Malcolm?"

The Choctaw nodded and replied, "No saw mill, neither, now that you ask. I know some folk there. Mostly Black Stick Choctaw. They wasn't the ones who noticed this trouble with the witness trees. As you just said, Pine Valley's way down the river and these hills are a real mess."

Longarm nodded and said, "Nearest white settlement would be about as far the other way, where the rails curve around the east slope of Rich Mountain at Mena, Arkansas. We've already decided the railroad runs all wrong for logging these here slopes and while there may or may not be any sort of a trail to Mena it has to cross the deep ravine of the Mountain Fork."

Malcolm told Fiona that one ran south to the Little Red River.

She said she knew that. So Longarm suggested they push on. That was one thing Fiona was able to agree on. She said she didn't want to be quoted on which of those three possible stumps might or might not be the missing witness tree. She said she was already in enough trouble. Longarm soothed, "Aw, come on, now that we know what we're looking for I'm sure we'll find an easier way to read buckeye stumps."

But they didn't. Up on the next rise where the map said they'd find the next bench mark they found it again, solid brass, driven into a big potato-shaped boulder of adobe-colored siltstone. As Fiona marked it triumphantly on her map Longarm nodded thoughtfully at the pound or more of brass pounded into the rock and decided, "It ain't petty theft or spitesome vandalism. Nobody seems out to really *hide* the Indian Nation from Arkansas. They've left bench-marked rocks and even oaks in place. It's almost as if someone's been at feud with buckeye trees for some fool reason."

Malcolm asked why. Longarm glanced skyward at the late afternoon sun before he replied, "If I knew that I'd have a better notion who's been doing it. Why don't you scout Roy up to help you fetch the ponies and such from that glade we left 'em in, old son? This old boulder will make us a handy fireback and it's best to camp on a dry rise like this one in such wet-looking woods."

The Chocktaw left, calling out in Muskogee for his pard as he vanished upslope amid the tanglewood. Fiona said, "We'd have run at least another mile before supper, had it been up to me."

He nodded but said, "I'd have helped, had we only had woods and them clouds from the south to concern us. But I can't help wondering about those three riders somewhere out there, or the other government men who entered these very woods earlier, and never came out."

155

She stared wide-eyed at the silence all about and murmured, "Brrr! But surely we'd have noticed, in such warm
weather, if anything bad had happened to anyone within
what, a mile?"

He shrugged and said, "Smells carry tricky in wooded
hills. I could swear I smelled wood smoke an hour or so
ago. But next time I sniffed it was gone and, like I said,
there ain't supposed to *be* any settlement for a good ten
miles in any direction."

Then, as if to make a liar of him, they both heard the
not-too-distant ringing of an axe on solid timber. It seemed
to be coming from a tad to their southwest, on the Indian
side of the survey line. Fiona wasn't wearing her Remington,
bless her trusting soul.

Longarm picked up the Winchester he'd leaned against
the handy boulder, levered a round into the chamber, and
handed it to her, advising, "Tote this polite, a pace behind
me, and let me do the talking."

She gulped and asked if it might not be safer to wait for
their Choctaw backing. He said, "You run back up the slope
if you want. I want to surprise our mysterious woodsman
before he notices all them pony hooves coming his way."

He started toward the sounds of wood chopping. Fiona followed, tight-lipped but more curious than scared. Longarm
stopped near a thick wall of alder, whispering, "They're just
the other side of this overgrown gullywash. Looking for a
gap could be looking for a load of number nine buck in
one's fool face. So I aim to work my way close and bull
through. I doubt there's more than two or three yards of
these alder whips blocking our way if we knuckle down."

She told him to go ahead. So he did. As they worked about
even with the axeman on the far side a reedy feminine voice
called out, *"Greas ort, a Hamish! A bheil thu sgith?"*

Fiona gasped and whispered, "She's speaking Gaelic! Not
Irish, though. It sounds more like Hebredian Scots!"

Longarm whispered, dryly, "I didn't think they were
jawing in Muskogee. Must be whites squatting on Indian

156

land, out this way where few would notice. What was she saying?"

Fiona explained, "She just told him to hurry up and asked if he was tired. It sounds as if someone's anxious to get home with some wood, no?"

The answer was yes. As Longarm simply grabbed a fistful of alder whips in either hand and stepped through, like Moses had stepped through the Red Sea, the large red-bearded lout who'd been cutting windfall into handier lengths froze, double axe in hand, as the little old lady by the pony cart behind him wailed, "Och, dinna murder us, kind sir! We've done ye nae wrong in the name of Our Laird Jesus!"

There was another good-sized youth on the narrow trail behind her, holding the halter of their stubby brown pony. A third brawny Scot, if Fiona was right, had been loading firewood in the cart from the rear. His hand dropped casually to the Patterson conversion riding on one hip. Longarm whipped his own .44-40 out but trained its muzzle polite as he called out, "Let's not get surly, folk. I'd be U.S. Deputy Custis Long and I carry no warrant on anyone answering to your description. So now it's your turn, right?"

As Fiona stepped through the alders behind him, with more effort, the old woman smiled toothlessly and called back, "We'd be the harmless an' homeless MacBeans, good sir. Poor auld Anna MacBean and her sweet Hamish, Angus, and Tavish. It was only firewood for our porridge we came here for, as anyone can see, and it's windfall we've taken."

Longarm put his sixgun away with a friendly nod, saying, "We don't hold timber rights on Indian land in any case, ma'am. I suppose you hadn't heard this was Indian land, of course?"

She looked as if she was about to blubber up on him as she protested they were only camped down by the river where nobody seemed to mind.

He said, "We might save us all a heap of hemming and hawing if I was to put my own cards on the table. Neither my sidekick, here, nor me are Indian agents. I told you nobody's sent me to arrest anyone for being named MacBean. I am in the market for information about three other white men in these parts, one wearing a white planter's hat and all three asking about me, that's Custis Long or maybe they'd call me Longarm?"

The old lady and her three literally big boys exchanged glances. The old lady shook her head and said, "You're the first strangers we've seen all summer. Nobody else seems to be dwelling around here, you see."

Longarm nodded and said, "You folk can dwell here all you like as far as we care. But I've one more question. Might you or anyone you know have any call to chop down buckeye trees in great numbers?"

The old lady seemed sincere as she replied, "Och, why?"

The one with the axe, closest to Longarm and Fiona, chimed in with, "I know what buckeyes are. Some Yankee kids offered me some to eat when we first crossed the main ocean. They're solid wood, like horse chestnuts."

The one holding the pony volunteered, in an even thicker brogue, "Och, I ken the sort of tree he means, Hamish! We've cut some up for firewood in the past and it burns bonnie anoo."

The old lady hushed him with a wave of her claw and almost whimpered, "Only *fallen* timber, good sir! We MacBeans would never harm a living *craobh!*"

Behind him, Fiona sweetly muttered something about Druids. Longarm called out, "I said I ain't after anyone on squatting or even moonshining charges, ma'am. You say you're camped further down, along the river?"

"Not all the way down by the running water," she explained. Then she added, "It floods, you see, in damp weather. Would you and your young friend care to join us for some humble broth and perhaps a bit of the creature?"

Longarm hesitated, torn between distaste and curiosity. They seemed harmless squatters, mayhaps brewing a few jars on their unrecorded claim as well. Longarm didn't care.

He understood why hardscrabble folk tending modest corn patches far from any town liked to convert some of it into something worth taking all the way in to sell. He was not alone in suspecting the ferocious federal excise on distilled liquor had been conceived by congressmen who'd rather tax the vices of others than their own ill-gotten gains. He glanced at Fiona—they still seemed to have her down as a soft-looking boy—and decided, "Well, we may as well be neighborly. But if you share your mountain dew with us you're going to have to let us leave you some sugar and salt ere we ride on."

The old lady cackled gleefully, told Hamish in English they had enough cordwood, and suggested they all get on down the mountain in time for supper. Longarm, Fiona, and two of the MacBean boys naturally strode the trail ahead of the cart as Angus led the pony and the old lady rode. Anyone afoot behind a pony cart was asking for shitty boots on such a narrow trail.

So Longarm and Fiona were striding side by side along the ruts, gazing ahead for some sign of the MacBean camp, cabin or whatever, when Hamish, still packing that big axe, casually called back, "*Cuin, Seanmhar? Is ullamh dhom. A bheil sinn?*"

So Fiona was already spinning around, eyes wide, as the old lady sweetly replied, "*Tha, bualeadh a nis.*" And then she was flat on her back atop the cordwood with Fiona's first round in her scrawny chest!

So Longarm shot Hamish just as the red-bearded rascal raised his big axe to strike. Old Hamish sure looked surprised he'd been killed, when one considered how ferocious he'd been *living,* up until then.

The pony bolted, spilling the old lady's corpse and lots of cordwood as it threw Longarm's aim off long enough for both Angus and Tavish to crash through that screen of alder whips just up the slope.

Longarm emptied the rest of his cylinder after them for luck, then he had Fiona and the Winchester down behind a

159

fallen cedar on the south side of the trail. She covered them both with the Winchester as he reloaded, dryly observing, "I take it they said something mean about us, just now?"

Fiona replied, still ashen-faced, "The one behind you with the axe said he was ready and asked why they were waiting. I knew what she was going to say, next. She still managed to tell them to jump us before I got her!"

Reloaded, Longarm removed his Stetson and risked a peek upslope. He couldn't see anything to shoot at. Nobody shot at him. Fiona asked what they ought to try next.

Longarm regarded the dead axeman and his sweet old momma, or maybe granny, it hardly mattered, as he told Fiona, "Nothing. By now Roy and Malcolm ought to be wondering about all that gunplay and, being Choctaw, they'll likely ease down behind those remaining MacBeans slicker than you or me could circle.

As if to prove his point they heard a distant plaintive voice call out, "*Cait a bheil thu, Tavish?*"

To which another voice replied, in an even more miserable tone, "*Seo, a doirteadh fola agus marbhanach!*"

Fiona explained, "Tavish says he's bleeding bad and dying, dear."

Longarm grimaced and said, "Bueno. Better him than us and now we know what likely happened to others ahead of us, don't we?"

Fiona repressed a shudder and replied, "They'd have done us in the same way, had I not grasped their intent just in time and all and all! They sounded so innocent, even as I was digesting their treacherous jabber!"

The wounded one called out again. There was no answer. Fiona said he was asking for someone to help him down the mountain so's he could die in bed like a Christian. There seemed to be no answers for Fiona to translate. Longarm had the wounded one figured off to their right a ways. That first call, asking where Tavish might be, in what sort of condition, had come from behind those alders and off to their left. When they heard a way more distant voice call out, in English, "Longarm? Miss Fiona?" he put down his pistol, cupped his hands to his mouth, and shouted, "Down here, Roy! There's two of 'em between us, both white, dressed ragged, and mean as snakes!"

Then he picked up his sixgun to whisper, "Stay here. Wait for our Choctaw boys to find you. Use that saddle gun on anybody else coming out of them alders."

Then he was up and beelining down the slope the other way, as fast as his long legs could lope him over windfall, ferns, and such. He doubted Roy and Malcolm would find both the surviving MacBeans between them and Fiona. He'd yelled that warning about two just in case he was wrong, and for Angus MacBean to hear no matter where in these woods he might be.

Longarm wasn't likely as sure where he was running, but he figured he had a head start on old Angus to begin with, while an exposed killer anxious to get home and pack up would be more apt to pussyfoot through the trees 'til he figured nobody could be staked out between hither and yon.

Longarm knew there could be more murderous MacBeans at home, but he didn't see how any he found there could know just what had happened to that dear old lady and her stalwart firewood gatherers. He didn't know for certain where the bottom of this infernal slope was, let alone which way he wanted to pop out of the tree line at the bottom. But then, running lickety-split, he heard a hound baying a tad to his left, or closer to the survey line than he'd have guessed. He veered that way, sixgun in hand, and saw more sunlight than shade on the green grass just ahead. So he was alert to all sorts of possibilities as he tore out into a considerable clearing to see quite a moonshining layout guarded by that mighty yapsome yard dog staked out between the cabin and the bigger still-shed on a long but secure-looking chain.

Longarm cut to his own left, watching the back windows of the cabin closer than he felt he had to watch a chained yard dog. His momentum carried him around to the back or

161

upslope side of the still shed. He rolled through a waist-high rear window to work his way around between the log wall and pot still—a big one hammered out of sheet copper by someone who really knew the whiskey trade.

He peered around the jamb of the front door opening. Neither the door nor windows of the still-shed amounted to more than openings cut through the log walls for air or access. From the deeply shaded opening, Longarm had the back door of the cabin covered. From this angle he could see they'd thrown up a pole corral and rambling log stable further down the slope. First things coming first and the distance being short, Longarm broke cover to cross the modest, bare distance in a downhill run that ended in his diving headfirst through a fortunately open window near the back door of the cabin.

He landed atop a dry sink piled with dishes, rolled on to land on his feet amid the falling crockery and snap, "Freeze in the name of the law!" before he noticed he seemed to have the place all to himself.

The cabin had been built one-room with a sleeping loft. It only took a few anxious moments to determine there was nobody holed up in the loft, either. So he popped out the front door to run on down to that stable.

That outbuilding's front entrance was only an open gap as well. He ducked inside and got some logs to his back as he swept the interior with his eyes and matching gun muzzle. That shaggy pony they'd had pulling their cart was staring back at him, traces dragging. It had shucked the cart somewhere along the way whilst loping home through the woods as spooked ponies usually would if they could.

There were four other ponies, bigger ones, more properly stalled. Outside, that yard dog had calmed a mite, but as if to make up for it one of the stalled ponies started trying to kick its way out 'til Longarm moved closer, sweet-talking it. He really meant what he'd said about hay and water 'til he heard that dog bark again, more in greeting than threat. So Longarm moved back to the opening and, sure

162

enough, down the slope came Angus MacBean, running as if he thought the hounds of hell were after him.

MacBean tore into the cabin through the back way before Longarm could decide how to handle it. He was still deciding when the burly but blubbering squatter tore right out the front door at him, packing a saddle with a roll and plenty of possibles lashed to it.

Longarm let MacBean lug his load almost to the stable door before he stepped out into the late sunlight with his gun and a smile to say, "Howdy, Angus. Sorry about your kin, but they started it, and now we're going to sort things out more sensible, ain't we?"

The big squatter squawked like a wild goose fixing to fly south and dropped his heavy saddle to the dust between them. But he froze when Longarm told him to freeze, in a less conversational tone.

MacBean sobbed, "Och, hae ye gaen daft, laddy? We meant ye nae harm. What did that other wi' ye tell ye aboot us?"

Longarm smiled thinly and said, "I could see Hamish aimed to chop somebody's head off. We're not going to get along at all if you keep bullshitting me, old son. So I'll deal you my cards face up in hopes of saving you more grasping at straws."

Angus insisted neither he nor his late family had done anything wrong. Longarm said, "I said to shut up and listen. As a federal lawman I could run you in for that pot still alone and, seeing it's bubbling away on Indian land I'd say Judge Parker up in Fort Smith could put you away for quite a spell for that alone."

Angus asked what a pot still was.

Longarm chuckled and said, "I told you all before your brother tried to brain me with that axe I wasn't a revenuer as a general rule. I'm more interested in more serious beeswax. I could even report I'd nailed the most likely killer or killers of those earlier government employees if you'd like to help me tidy up some loose ends before you just ride on, Angus."

163

MacBean stared back with dawning hope and allowed he was awfully tidy as a rule, adding, "It was ever Hamish wi' the axe, *ye ken*. Me and poor Tavish may hae helped a wi' bit wi' the ones wha kept twitching but . . ."

"Let's not talk about killing folk to keep 'em from reporting your moonshining and I won't have to talk too much about which way you might have ridden when we parted friendly," Longarm cut in. "I really want to know who cut down those witness trees, and why."

MacBean seemed sincerely ignorant as he took his time, with Longarm's help, recalling that yes he and his brothers had salvaged some fallen timber that might have been nut-wood and could have been cut down by humankind rather than time and the mountain winds. But, even trying to wriggle off the hook, and he seemed to be wriggling indeed, the murderous moonshiner couldn't come up with even an educated guess as to who might have felled those trees along the survey line. He said he had indeed noticed fresh blazes with some sort of lettering incised on the exposed wood. He hadn't paid any attention, not knowing how to read or write. He finally recalled his granny saying something about the border of the Indian Nation being somewhere in these parts and someone likely marking trees accordingly. Angus said she hadn't known how to read and write, either. Nobody in the murderous clan had struck Longarm as awesomely bright.

He knew that despite how highfalutin it might sound, lots of old-timey country folk used Roman numerals in lieu of the harder-to-fathom Arabic numerals modern schoolkids were taught. More than one log barn or even house frame erected by self-taught country carpenters still bore the simpler numerals the Romans had doubtless inherited from yet earlier times, as easy as it was to scribe an I, a V, or an X.

Longarm decided, "All right. Let's say you squatters here had nothing to do with that old survey line and simply acted natural when strangers rode in to question you about it. Whether we lay all the blame on your dead kin or not, I'm going to have to produce me some bodies when I report I had to gun some murderers, see?"

Angus said their Seanmhar had insisted they be neat about anyone Hamish might have to axe. They were all buried too deep for flies or foxes to get at, hither and yon up the mountain. When Longarm said he'd have to do better than that Hamish moaned, *"Och,* I knew ye never meant to keep faith wi' me, ye perfidious *sassunach!"*

So Longarm shot him before he could get that pocket derringer all the way out. Hamish landed spread-eagle on his back a few paces away, staring back up at Longarm with a petulant expression, as if he'd been punished for just trying to have a little fun.

Longarm said, "Yep, I never meant to let you go. But I wouldn't have gunned you if you hadn't made me, just now."

Hamish didn't answer. Men seldom did when they'd been shot in the heart at such close range their shirt front still smoldered, wet as it was.

Longarm made sure the ponies had some water to last them but left the disposal of Angus and that yard dog for later as he legged it back up the slope to where he'd left Fiona and, with any luck, three dead MacBeans and two live Choctaw. Getting up took longer than getting down.

He found Roy and Malcolm about where he'd expected to, near that log he'd left Fiona and his Winchester waiting. The Choctaw had hauled Tavish MacBean out on the trail. He'd been truthful about all that bleeding he'd been bitching about. A lucky round had hulled his left lung and he'd bled to death all down the front of his fool self.

Fiona was nowhere to be seen. When Longarm asked where she might be Malcolm said they'd just been talking about that. They hadn't found her where Longarm had left her, or anywhere else, for that matter.

Chapter 18

They whooped and they hollered and they searched for signs as the shadows got ever longer. Roy Kenowa found what might have been the mark of Fiona's bitty boot heel in a patch of bare clay, aiming south the way Longarm had lit out after Angus MacBean. Longarm considered that before he decided, "Had she run after me she'd have caught up long ere now. Had she hurt herself along the way I'm pretty sure I'd have spied her, coming back up the slope through the trees."

Malcolm opined, "There was no signs of struggle around yonder log. A body can walk over forest duff without leaving tracks. It's another tale entire when a gal's drug kicking and screaming."

Roy pointed out, "We'd have heard any kicking and screaming. We found that lung-shot bastard dead, up the other side of them alders. Longarm and the gal left them other two dead on along the trail and tracked that last one down. So who was left to grab Miss Fiona?"

Longarm sighed and said, "Those three white riders who were looking for us back in Page, that's who, and I ought to be whipped with snakes for leaving Fiona here with only a loaded Winchester to protect her!"

Malcolm soothed, "She never went down fighting with no saddle gun in her hands. The only way it works is say somebody got the drop on her and frog-marched her off at gunpoint whilst the rest of us were so busy with these murderous moonshiners!"

Longarm holstered his reloaded sixgun, started to reach for a smoke, and decided not to as he said, "We won't find her here. If she lit out on her own she ought to be down by the MacBean spread or back in our own camp. I take it you boys brought the ponies and such up by that big potato rock before you run down this way, afoot, to see what all that shooting might have been about?"

Malcolm said they sure had. Roy thought it more likely the gal had been grabbed than that she'd run off for no good reason.

Longarm sighed, glanced up at the sunset-gilded tree tops all around, and decided, "Either way, we got to tidy up before we study on supper. Let's see, we got these three dead bodies up this way and I left old Angus dead in his own dooryard. There's livestock to be taken care of as well as likely more evidence down by their pot still. So what say we find the pony cart that has to be hung up somewheres around here. Then we can load these three aboard and manhandle it on down easy enough."

The Choctaw didn't argue. But Roy asked about Fiona and of course their own stock. Longarm nodded and said, "You're right. We'd best go back up to that potato rock and, whether she's there or not, gather up our own stock and gear. That way, we can have everything down the mountain and forted up behind stout log walls whilst we ponder what in blue blazes is going on around here!"

They left the dead lying for now and bulled back through those alders to trudge on up through the trees in the gathering dusk. Roy said they'd be lucky if they had themselves set up down at the MacBean spread before starbright. Longarm said he knew the way and that he was more worried about Fiona. But when Roy started calling ahead to her, Longarm growled, "Don't tell anyone you're coming, old son. Make 'em guess."

The Choctaw gulped and said, "Sweet Jesus! What'll we do if they have our camp staked out?"

Longarm replied, "Make 'em tell us where the gal is, for openers. We'd best fan out and move on in line of skirmish. I don't have to tell either of you where that big rock is, do I?"

He didn't. The two Choctaw were young and newer than Longarm to manhunting, but the skills they'd picked up trailing nervous deer and sly old coons through their native hills stood them in good stead as, working together but spread far apart, they closed in on their campsite by that prominent landmark to find nobody there but their tethered ponies. Longarm circled the big potato-shaped rock for signs as the Choctaw started packing all they had to move on down to the MacBean spread.

The light was getting poor. But at least the slanting rays of the setting sun served to etch every high or low spot orange or purple. He spied what might have been a heel print, where he felt sure Fiona had never trod in his presence. He dropped to one knee for a better look just as someone fired from cover in the middle distance to spang shattered rock all over him from the lee side!

He'd flopped flat and commenced to sidewind, of course, as a second shot rang out, powdering his nose with fine grit and bits of shattered lead. So he knew he was done for as he peered about in vain for even a shred of cover, knowing his invisible assailant had him dead to rights against that big smooth boulder with the sunset lighting up his exposed ass.

So he winced considerable when he heard two more shots in rapid succession from the same direction. Then he noticed he was still alive, after all, and some total stranger was calling out, "You by the rock! Might you be Deputy Long from out Denver way?"

Longarm called back, "I sure am. Who might *you* be, you bushwhacking son of a bitch?"

The same voice called back, "Aw, I ain't no son of a bitch, I'm Deputy Orville Gaynor out of Fort Smith. We just got the sneaky cuss who had you in his sights. Noticed him set up ahint a stump out here and so we were watching to see what happened next when you come along and, well . . . Thunderation! Look what we just shot in the back whilst she was trying to shoot another lawman in the back!"

Longarm was afraid he knew, but he still hoped he was wrong until he'd joined the three men further out in the trees, one of them wearing a white planter's hat. They were standing over a smaller form sprawled facedown amid the ferns, Longarm's Winchester nearby. Fiona's hat had fallen off, exposing her long hair. Longarm had to stop near a shaggy hickory, lean against it, and vomit mostly green taste before he felt up to moving closer. Deputy Gaynor, the one in the white hat, said, "Howdy. Judge Parker sent us after you to back your play as soon as he got in from Little Rock. You sure have been a hard man to find. Nobody we've asked along the way had seen hide nor hair of you."

Another deputy piped up, "It's a good thing we heard all them gunshots, starting a good spell back. How come this gal dressed up like a man took to blazing away at you so much, pard?"

Longarm replied, "Why do you think I just now puked? I thought she was with *me* and, for just a moment there, I suspected she'd tricked me into a God-awesome mistake."

He struck a match to light a cheroot. He was sorry he had as he got a better look at Fiona's crumpled form. You wouldn't have thought anyone so petite could have had so much blood in her. But the three-for-a-nickel smoke served to get his spit back aboard his sandpaper tongue as he shook out the match, saying, "She must have been sincerely on my side when the shooting *started*. I just tricked a confession out of a moonshiner who'd been mad at the both of us. Finding herself alone with that Winchester during the confusion, she

169

must have seen she'd never have a better chance to backshoot me and lay the blame on others."

By this time they'd been joined by the two Choctaw. Longarm introduced them to the Fort Smith lawmen and vice versa. When he'd tersely explained what Miss Fiona was doing down there at their feet Malcolm swallowed and said, "Well I never. No offense, Longarm, but we had the impression she was sort of sweet on you."

Longarm said, "Let's not speak ill of the dead. Whether she liked me or not I suspect she was commencing to be vexed by the way I kept pushing her to run her survey. You heard how she kept saying jobs like her'n were tough for a she-male to get and how intent she was on an outstanding survey."

Deputy Gaynor said, "They told us up at Fort Smith about her boss, the one they'd really hired to resurvey this line, getting backshot by a person or persons unknown. Do you reckon we've just solved that mystery?"

Longarm took a deep drag on his cheroot to give himself more time to think. He let it out and decided, "There's still some missing pieces. I sent some wires before we left Fort Smith. Time we get back there I ought to have some answers. I'd like to know a mite more about the late Captain Boyle and his real love life before I'd be willing to bet a month's pay. But, just guessing, I can see how this sweet little two-face could have gunned him in the lot betwixt the river and their hotel in the wee small hours, rolled him and his personal baggage into the current to be carried north around that big oxbow, and pegged a shot at me, later, as I arrived."

Longarm had warned them not to, but Roy Kenowa just couldn't seem to contain himself as he blurted, "That makes no sense at all, Longarm! What you and her have been up to in your sleeping bag more than once is neither here nor there, but she surely wasn't trying to *kill* you!"

Longarm smiled thinly and replied, "I'll be the judge of that. But you may have just answered your own question, Roy. If you two could hear a little heavy breathing you'd have surely noticed gunshots and she just wasn't big enough to strangle me."

Orville Gaynor proclaimed, "Had we not come along she'd have had you redskins backing her tale of woe after she backshot Longarm from over here and staggered into camp an hour or so later, without this murder weapon, to find both you boys forted up against them trash whites and doubtless glad to see she was still alive after all that running for her life and honor through this tanglewood."

Longarm said, "That's about the size of it. Now we'd best gather all our forces together, coffee up, and get cracking with all the scattered bodies. The only one of the moonshiners I got anything like the truth out of told me his murdersome kin had planted them other federal employees hither and yon amid all these infernal trees."

Orville Gaynor waved eastward and said, "We left our own ponies ahint some loblolly when we figured we'd rid close enough to all that gunfire. We're going to need *dogs* to find buried folk under this forest duff, even by daylight."

One of his own men suggested the pack of redbone hounds at that homestead they'd passed that very morning. Gaynor said, "Worth a try, if you want to ride over yonder, Luke. But seeing their owner bragged on their noses I'll bet that local sheriff's posse has already beat us to 'em."

Longarm said he hadn't heard about any other lawmen chasing any other outlaws in these parts. So Gaynor explained, "Homicide case. Not our jurisdiction. Sheriff of Polk County, Arkansas, wants a hired hand for murdering an old beekeeper and preserving him in beeswax."

The deputy who'd suggested the hunting hounds snorted and said, *"Trying* to, you mean. Nobody'd seen the poor old beekeeper for some time. His hired hand kept telling visitors he was sick in bed."

Longarm blinked and demanded, "Hold on! Are we talking about an old crippled gent named Beverwick and a dimwit called Tiny?"

Gaynor said, "Yep. Sold honey down by the railroad tracks near the Indian Nation line. Neighbor with a keener nose than most dropped by more'n once about money old Beverwick owed. Smelled more than a rat, despite all that beeswax, and flagged down a train to take the suspicion to the county seat at Mena."

Another deputy volunteered, "Hired hand must have suspected his game was up. Sheriff and some riders got right over there, by railroad flat car, only to find the killer long gone. Understand they wired the Indian Police to keep an eye out for him, too."

Longarm shook his head wearily and said, "I must be getting old. I never suspected Tiny of two-facing me, neither. We'd best all coffee up before we fan out, boys. I suspicion we got us a heap of dreary chores to tend to, hear?"

Chapter 19

It took them all night and a good part of the next morning before they had everyone planted shallow and coated with lime in a neat row near the MacBean cabin. They knew some kith and kin of anyone not born a MacBean might eventually want to reclaim rags and bones they had coming. So they laid them a decent distance apart and marked each one with a cedar roof shingle inscribed with an awl and gone over in pencil.

Those redbone hounds and their teenaged owner had been a big help with the more smellsome but already planted bodies out in the woods. The homestead boy, a harelip called Bunny (it didn't seem to bother him) said the posse had indeed been by, before anyone with Longarm had called on him and his redbones. But the sheriff's boys had already recruited some bloodhounds and they'd been fixing to turn back in any case. For the bloodhounds had failed to pick up Tiny's scent on the Arkansas side of the line and the sheriff hadn't wanted any trouble with those sullen Choctaw.

Malcolm Wetumka had protested his folk weren't all that sullen but wondered aloud whether his kinsman, Jacob, had jurisdiction over a white boy wanted for killing another white outside the Indian Nation.

Longarm said to ask old Orville. The Fort Smith lawman nodded and replied, "Any peace officer anywhere can hold a suspect 'til his lawyer shows up with a writ or a lawman who does have jurisdiction shows up to collect the cuss."

Malcolm said in that case Tiny was good as caught. No white boy was about to elude old Jacob and his Choctaw posse on Choctaw hunting grounds.

Orville Gaynor opined it didn't matter to any paid-up federal lawman. He asked Longarm what they were supposed to do next. Longarm supressed a yawn and said, "Get at least four hours worth of shut-eye. We've done all we can down this way. I'll carry Miss Fiona's gear and such survey notes as she made back to Fort Smith with you. I ain't qualified to complete her survey but, what the hell, a rough estimate ought to hold everyone 'til the government can do it right. It ain't like anyone's struck gold or even filed a homestead claim smack on the fool line."

Malcolm said, "I can't even see why someone cut down all them buckeye trees."

So naturally Longarm had to tell the Fort Smith deputies about the mysterious malice someone in these parts seemed to feel for timber of modest value bearing inedible nuts.

Gaynor agreed it was mysterious, adding, "All I recall about buckeye trees is that they must have a mess of 'em growing in Ohio if they call Ohio the Buckeye State."

Longarm nodded absently and said, "I've been going over everything I've ever heard or read about the species. I read in bed now and again when I find myself alone in a strange town. It ain't any more silly than jacking off. Miss Fiona and me were jawing about such selective cutting whilst she was still behaving more friendly and she had her a degree in botany."

He took a thoughtful drag on the cheroot he was smoking and mused, "I know she wasn't in cahoots with the murdersome MacBeans, here. I doubt she could have been in with the party or parties unknown behind all that nut tree logging. For openers she had an alibi. She was back home in Saint Lou when said trees were cut. All the exposed wood had weathered a couple of winters or more. She acted sincerely puzzled as the rest of us, too."

Malcolm pointed out, "She acted like she liked you, a lot, right?"

Longarm wrinkled his nose and said, "That's easier for a woman to fake and even a man can feel inspired by a pretty enemy for a spell as he waits for a chance to doublecross her. I'd like to think she was trying to convince me I should give her more time for her survey run. If I'm right about the murder of Captain Boyle she was more interested in her chosen career than killing anyone."

Malcolm said Roy had a pot on the stove in the MacBean cabin. As they headed that way Longarm was musing, half to himself, "Aesculus something, they call the buckeye in botany books. Comes in more than one closely related species as a big shrub or fair-sized tree. Soft, white but durable wood. Sensible choice for a witness tree. Fruit's almost a dead ringer for the European horse chestnut. Nobody but a horse would want to eat neither so what *else* do we recall about the damned old buckeye?"

Gaynor said it sounded mighty uninteresting, so far.

Longarm nodded, let out some smoke, and recalled, "Blooms pretty along the Ohio in the spring. Big clusters of red, white, or yellow flowers along about Maytime."

Gaynor asked, "How come? So many colors, I mean. Seems to me fruit or nut trees ought to bloom one damn color or another."

Longarm explained, "I just said there's more'n one kind of buckeye. Kissing kin trees bear slightly different flowers. That's what makes 'em so interesting from an Ohio paddle wheeler. Be more tedious passing mile after mile of white,

175

yellow, or even red flowers and, hold on, I just recalled something about them flowers. Was it the red ones, the white ones, or . . . Never mind, it would hardly matter to a half-wit. You boys finish up here. I'll thank you to get all the camping and survey possibles back where they belong. I got to ride, traveling light!"

Malcolm protested, "What about that coffee? What about that sleep you said you needed?"

Longarm was already running for the corral, but he was polite enough to call back, "Ain't got time. Got to catch up with that poor half-wit Tiny before anyone can shut him up forever!"

Chapter 20

He did, but it wasn't easy. Both Longarm and Captain Boyle's big bay were branch-whipped and lathered by the time they'd beelined catty-corner up and over Rich Mountain Ridge and down into the powwow still going on in Page.

He had to dismount and weave his way across the street afoot to get to the police station next to the barber without running down any basket dancers. Young gals dancing in circles with baskets over their heads didn't have the least notion where they were reeling or who they might be bumping into so gigglesome.

He found the same Choctaw lawman, Jacob, inside with plenty of company. Longarm was pleased to see most wore federal badges and all looked reasonably Indian, braids or not. Jacob said, "You sure got here fast, Longarm. We just now captured that Arkansas killer and I hadn't even wired my brag to Polk County, yet!"

Longarm said, "I had more faith in you. So I didn't wait for no brag. I'd be much obliged if you'd hold off wiring anyone before I've had a chance to talk to him, Jacob."

The Indian nodded but said, "How come? Killing Mr. Beelzebub and slathering him with beeswax was mean as hell, but hardly federal."

Longarm said, "Fooling with federal survey lines is. I'd like your deposition as a federal witness, too."

The big Indian rose to lead Longarm into their cell block. Along the way Longarm brought Jacob up-to-date on the case so far. At a solid boilerplate door the Choctaw drew his antique, thumb-busting .45 with one hand while he unlocked the door with the other, saying, "Watch your step with this big moose. He gave us quite a struggle, hauling him in through the tanglewood. I'd be feeling desperate if I was him right now, too."

But on the far side of the door they found the giant in bib overalls curled up like a big scared baby in one corner of the steel-walled patent cell. As the Indian lawman lounged in the doorway Longarm sat on the fold-down cot, holding out a cheroot to the prisoner.

Tiny didn't take it. He blubbered, "I never! I swear I never! He just went to sleep one night and wouldn't wake up the next morn. I did what I could for him. Mr. Beverwick was more than a daddy to me. For he never hit me like my real folk did."

"Why did you cover him up with beeswax, then?" asked Jacob, one eyebrow raised.

Tiny sobbed, "I had to do something when he started smelling bad, didn't I? Mr. Beverwick told me about the bees doing that to say a dead bird or mouse they'd stung to death inside a wild hive. He said beeswax kept dead critters from rotting. I reckon he must have meant *little* critters, like birds and mice, though. After a while he stunk like anything, no matter how much wax I melted and poured over him."

"Some of him likely leaked into his mattress," Longarm opined in a soothing tone. Then he added, "Mr. Beverwick told you all sorts of things about bees and what might be good or bad for 'em, right?"

When the giant nodded and repeated that the late Mr. Beverwick had been awesomely smart about everything, Longarm said, "Bueno. I got to question you with care lest they accuse me of putting words in your mouth. So I'm asking you to tell us about buckeye trees, Tiny."

The big kid brightened some and said, "The ones Mr. Beverwick and me were worried about have wicked flowers. I forget whether he said they poison the bees or their honey." Then he clapped both hands to his ever-wet lips and just stared wide-eyed.

Longarm lit the cheroot, seeing nobody else seemed to want to smoke it, and soothed, "There's no need to keep secrets your boss told you to keep, now that he's gone on to that great beehive in the sky, old son. Anyone can see two men cut 'em down with that whipsaw. Was it after such a hard day's work he suffered his first brain stroke?"

Jacob muttered, "Careful. It's best not to prompt 'im."

Longarm nodded and said, "Forget that last question, Tiny. I'd best put things another way and leave it up to such a bright old boy to decide. I told you when last we talked why I was down this way. You told me, then, you knew nothing about anyone cutting down witness trees and I respect a boy who can follow the orders of a boss who's been good to him. I don't know whether Mr. Beverwick died natural or some other way. I ain't a judge. I could take you before a federal judge in Fort Smith who's firm but fair and you could tell him your whole tale, at a properly conducted trial with no cussing or interrupting allowed. But I can only take you in as a federal prisoner if you've committed a federal offense. Otherwise Jacob, here, will have to turn you over to Polk County and I hope you can find a jury of your peers willing to listen as you explain all that hot wax you poured over that old man, dead or alive."

Tiny gulped and said, "They'll hang me like a dog, if I'm lucky. I'd way rather go up to Fort Smith with you. I hear Judge Parker spares some boys who've done wrong and that even when he don't his hangman, Prince Maledon, gets it over quick and painless."

Longarm said, "I doubt you'd hang for what you done, Tiny. Seeing you were only following orders, you might get off with as little as six months."

Tiny nodded eagerly and said, "It was Mr. Beverwick said to cut them buckeyes lest they sicken his bees and, like you said, it can't hurt him to tell you, now."

Longarm asked whose grand notion it had been to mark other trees more or less along the same north-south line. Tiny repeated what he'd said about the beekeeper's cleverness. The old illiterate might well have thought he was helping. Longarm made a mental note to remind Judge Parker it had been the boss, not the even dumber hired hand, who'd thought meaningless Romanesque numerals on out-of-line trees would do the job. He glanced up at Jacob, who nodded and said, "I'd say you've got most of it put together. But let's see if I got it straight in my Choctaw brain."

Counting on his fingers, Jacob said, "In the beginning, before Beverwick took sick and everyone else had an alibi, the beekeeper and this boy, who'd have never got a job with anyone else, messed up that old survey line to improve their bee business and that's where they can be set aside."

He grabbed a second finger and continued, "Some of us ignorant savages saw someone had fiddled with our borders, suspected another land grab, and commenced to raise hell. So the survey service sent some old boys to double-check, they tripped over that MacBean bunch, and the moonshiners killed 'em, thinking they were revenuers?"

Longarm nodded and said, "The deputies who rode down along the line after 'em, too. The MacBeans might have got Fiona Coyne and me as well if she hadn't savvied their sneaky ways."

The Indian counted another finger, deciding, "*She* was sneaky as well. When Captain Boyle was sent on *his* mission he asked for her because she was a botanist as well and he hoped she'd know more than him about witness trees, up or down."

Longarm nodded and said, "She says he made a play for her. He might have. She might have simply wanted his job. She *got* it when he was found dead way north of town. I suspect she killed him in the overgrown lot near their hotel in the wee small hours and rolled him into the nearby river. The current carried him north, along that big oxbow, and Lord only knows what happened to his personal baggage. She hung on to the surveying gear he'd have likely kept in his room, not the hotel stable, where anyone might have stolen it. The buffalo gun she used on him might have been his, too. She tried to use it on me and then threw it in the weeds near her hotel when she noticed how hard I was to murder. When she noticed how friendly I was she might have hoped to let me live. She'd have handed in a crackerjack survey with my help had I been just a tad more helpsome. I reckon she figured, once I'd taken care of the dangerous MacBeans for her, she'd be able to redraw her maps, her way, without as much lip from Roy and Malcolm."

Jacob started to count on another finger. Then he blinked and said, "Son of a bitch, I can't come up with any more questions! Like I said, you've put it together perfect!"

Longarm shrugged modesty and said, "I'll want to make certain Boyle's wife never headed east to join him. All bets are off if it turns out him and me were both led astray by another wicked lady entire. But the more I consider the less I can pin his murder on anyone but Fiona Coyne. She dressed sort of mannish all the time. With a travel duster and her hat crown creased different she'd fit better than any other gal I met along the way as the one who delivered a fake telegram to Boyle, just to get him outside, and then pegged a round at me the next day, disguised as mannish."

Jacob nodded and said, "I'm satisfied and it ain't as if anyone but this poor simp will ever stand trial, on a minor charge. So I reckon he's all yours, pard."

Longarm stared wearily down at the huge but likely harmless prisoner and said, "Seeing I beat Polk County to him, damn near killing myself and my mount in the process, I reckon it won't hurt to leave him on ice in here 'til I tend my pony, repair the damage to me as well, and catch at least a few hours' shut-eye. I don't suppose you got a hotel here in Page, old son?"

The Indian laughed incredulously and said, "I admire a white man with a dry sense of humor. But I know more than one lady of the nominal Choctaw persuasion who might be persuaded to put you up for a spell."

Longarm rose, told Tiny to keep the faith, and asked Jacob to aim him the right way. The Indian hesitated, then asked, "Ah, just how sleepy might you really be, Longarm?"

To which his white visitor could only reply, "That depends on what she might look like, if that's what you're asking."

It was, and Miss Sadie Ninneka said she'd never forget him when he rode on with his prisoner in his own good time.

Watch for

LONGARM AND THE ARIZONA SHOWDOWN

157th in the bold LONGARM series
from Jove

Coming in January!